Joey, a Lebanese father of two, living in Dubai, has always been a storyteller. He started off by reading bedtime stories to his children and then moved on to creating his own stories where the kids were the protagonists.

Being a veteran advertising and marketing person, Joey is well known for his creative ideas and strategic thinking allowing him to build stories for brands through his advertising and marketing career. This inspired him to write stories for his own children building on his family's nickname "The Bears" in his hometown of Brummana.

To my wife and kids, for being the best story I can ever tell.

Joey Tawil

THE LAST OF THE BEAR TRIBE

AUSTIN MACAULEY PUBLISHERS™

LONDON • CAMBRIDGE • NEW YORK • SHARJAH

ISBN – 9789948776307 – (Paperback)
ISBN – 9789948776314 – (E-Book)

Application Number: MC-10-01-1834284
Age Classification: E

Printer Name: iPrint Global Ltd
Printer Address: Witchford, England

First Published 2023
AUSTIN MACAULEY PUBLISHERS FZE
Sharjah Publishing City
P.O Box [519201]
Sharjah, UAE
www.austinmacauley.ae
+971 655 95 202

The design of the cover was made by Waqas Saeed

Chapter 1
Who Am I?

It was a very cold morning when Sam woke up, startled from a dream. He had seen knights battling on a field with blood and gore everywhere. He opened his eyes to look around when the pain in his head shot like a hot knife searing through his brain. He winced and slowly tried opening his eyes again. His vision was blurred, and his hearing was muffled with the exception of the deafening ringing sound in his head.

As he slowly tried lifting himself, he realized that he was lying on the ground in a large meadow and around him were the bodies of thousands of knights, dead. His dreams were actually memories of the previous day. But Sam could not remember who he was and how he got there. More importantly, he had no clue where "there" was and when! Besides his name, Sam remembered almost nothing else.

Sam slowly stumbled to his feet and took two steps to the right of the seemingly senior officer's body lying next to him. Sam guessed he was senior as the officer's tail was adorned with a golden tail-lace which showed the insignia of his family crest. Tail-laces were only allowed for officers in the Kiaff army and above. How he knew that, was a question he could not answer. After all, Kiaff and Vegna were neighboring kingdoms and the people of both sides looked exactly the same! Sam looked down at his body to see he was not wearing a soldier's uniform, but a long tunic with no leggings. He assumed that the leggings had been stolen by battlefield robbers who usually wait for the battle to end and then rush in to steal what they could find on the dead.

Not sure which way to go, Sam decided to walk north and see if he could find another living soul to ask for information. As it was early morning, Sam was able to identify east and walk to his left. The larger of the two suns was right at the horizon and the smaller one was yet to rise. This gave the land a beautiful orange haze which was called by both kingdoms *shafaq*. During shafaq, animals would leave their burrows and wander aimlessly in the forests giving the hunters little to no challenge; meaning that food was always in abundance for all. But when the large sun or "amoon" was right above the land, and the smaller one "upshee" was risen, animals gained super speed and strength, meaning they could not be hunted.

Sam walked slowly in the forest until he found a track which he assumed would lead to a village or a camp. He followed it cautiously, as he was not sure where he stood in the war and if he was known to have been on any side of the battle.

It had been a few hours since Sam started walking down that road before he saw a blur moving in the bushes near him. The creature moved so fast; Sam was not able to make out its color, let alone the species. With the super speed, he guessed it was already noon. For his safety from the super-fast and strong animals, Sam walked in the middle of the road to give himself the extra nanosecond of advantage should one of those creatures decide to run through him! As he centered his steps, he felt the air go damp and the humidity rising sharply. His muffled hearing was slowly clearing, and he was sure he could hear the sound of running water. There was a small ascent before him and as he climbed it, he saw a gushing river pass by. He had followed the path to the river.

At the riverbed, he saw young ladies washing clothes and bathing. But there was no one guarding them. *In a time of war, these people must be very stupid or brave to let their females about without any defenses!* he thought to himself, but before he got to finish his thought completely, he heard a strong call from the river, one of the women noticed him and shouted to the others.

In a span of two breaths, the women had joined together in what looked like a battle configuration and each of them had a club in her hand and they stared at Sam without blinking. Sam felt his mouth dry and wanted to run, but his feet betrayed him, and he just stood still.

The leader of the women, a tall blond woman, walked slowly towards him. Her tail-lace caught the sun and reflected in Sam's eyes. It was gold, so he immediately knew she was of royal descent. He slowly started moving towards her as if in a trance, captivated by her beauty, her flowing hair, her purple eyes and exceptionally fit figure. Then, they stood, eye to eye, Sam and Jemma.

--

Lya was busy tidying up the tavern from last night's concert when she heard the commotion outside. She put down the bag of rubbish that was in her hand and walked out to see what was going on. As she walked out through the Inn's door,

11

she saw Darryl in a fist fight with Ben. Ben was the town's champion boxer and was taunting Darryl with jabs to the face. Darryl had a cut on his right cheek, and it looked like he was about to cry. Lya, being Darryl's sister, stepped in with a thundering blow to Ben's left cheek throwing him off balance and knocking him off his feet.

"Leave my brother alone or the next one will blind you!" she roared.

Ben looked up at her, smiled and said, "Only a wife can cause this much damage and threat for more!"

Ben got up, dusted himself and walked to Lya who was checking Darryl's cheek, and said, "We were just playing, honey, no need to be so defensive."

Lya smiled at Ben, and said, "Even though he is my elder brother and your childhood friend, he is still the treasurer of the council and a respected person in Sanctuary, you need to be reminded of that, honey." She smiled and as usual Ben was putty in her hands. He smiled back, kissed her and both walked into the inn to finish cleaning up. Darryl followed in, slapped Ben on the back and pointing to Lya, said, "If she hadn't saved you, I was going to get mad!" Ben smiled back and the trio went on to clean the tavern.

A few minutes later, the inn's door swung open, and a stranger walked in. She was blond, tall and had a golden tail-lace. Behind her walked a handsome fellow, very muscular and sporting a ponytail. They both had purple eyes and looked like a fearsome couple. The tall lady sat at the bar and asked for ale while the muscular gentleman sat beside her and remained silent. Lya was completely taken aback by the handsome man and felt as if she knew him, but she decided she would not bring this point to light as she was not sure.

Ben, being surprised at the two strangers' appearance and the gigantic muscles on the man, wanted to mark his territory and started talking to them.

"Where are you from," he asked the man.

Sam could not answer this question as he was still not sure. So, he thought of the simplest answer, "anywhere and everywhere."

Being unsatisfied with the answer, Ben decided to push further, "So Kiaff and Vegna?" he said laughing, "Must be confusing for you."

Sam paid no attention to Ben's jibe and remained silent, which infuriated Ben. "ANSWER ME WHEN I TALK TO YOU!" Ben screamed as he raised his hand to smack Sam.

From the corner of her eye, Lya saw Jemma twitch and a sudden flash of ruby red appeared and disappeared with it. Ben's raised hand flew and landed on the Inn's door with a thud.

With a quiet demeanor Jemma said, "Don't raise your hand at those who can crush you."

Darryl was watching all this and decided to help his old friend, so he walked over to where Sam was still sitting at the bar with Ben slumped down next to him on the floor and tried to lift Ben to take him to the healer. As he bent to pick up Ben, Darryl saw that part of a large ghastly scar on Sam's right leg showing from under his tunic as Sam was still not wearing any leggings. Darryl remembered a story of the warrior clan that was wiped out many years ago and the rumor that the chief's children escaped, but the son was badly hurt in the right thigh. *It couldn't be him*, Darryl thought to himself. *A child of that age would not have survived this long on his own.*

Pushing the thought from his mind, Darryl lifted Ben, carried his friend's severed hand, and walked out of the tavern.

"Does this place help with your memory?" Jemma asked Sam.

"Not sure. Some smells seem familiar, but not a familiar shape or face." He answered emotionlessly.

"Then we better keep moving," Jemma said, "you can stay with our tribe for a while."

Sam nodded and they both got up to leave. From behind the bar, Lya could see that these two seemed to be from a unique breed, the likes of which she had not seen in years. "Excuse me," she said. As she said it, she immediately regretted speaking as she was not sure what to say next! Both warriors turned to her and looked in silence. Lya gathered her thoughts and eventually spoke out. "We have had some raiders come to our town and ransack it at least once a week. Seeing that the two of you look like trained warriors, can we ask you for your help in fighting them back?" Jemma swung her tail to show the jewelry on it to Lya, giving the message that she is a high-ranking officer, but Sam had already responded with "Sure!" Jemma turned and met Sam's eyes, they looked at each other for a second and then Jemma said, "Why not!"

Lya's inn above the tavern was made of pine wood and had a constant smell of fresh pine. Sam did not care much for the scent but Jemma thought that this is what heaven smelt like. They were offered a single room, but they politely asked for separate rooms. The last two days traveling together had made it clear that they have the sort of friendship that is real and neither of them saw the other in a romantic way, although the few people they met on the road thought they were a couple.

On the third day of being in Sanctuary, the raiders came. Sam and Jemma were sitting enjoying the cool breeze and a cool ale on the porch by the inn when the raiders' dust appeared on the horizon.

"Shall we do this?" Jemma asked Sam.

"Sure," was his reply. Sam and Jemma stood side by side at the main entrance of town, behind them was about twenty of the townsfolk, men and women, who were holding pitchforks and clubs. Lya was in the second row with Darryl, while Ben was watching from a distance with his right hand reattached but still bandaged and weak. Lya then realized that neither Sam nor Jemma had any weapons with them. She was about to call out to them when she saw them both raise their right arms a bit and weapons materialized in them from thin air. Sam had a battle-axe with double sided blades. It shined blue in the shade as if it was sapphire that caught the sun, and in the center of the shaft was a red line that looked like it was made of fire. The fire line shaped into an inscription that read: '*Son of man, slayer of demons*' and Jemma had a sleek sword in her hand. The sword was blood red as if made from ruby stones and on the blade was an inscription that said: '*Daughter of queens, slayer of men.*'

--

Jake was feeling extra confident in today's raid. He had been practicing his fighting techniques and was sure he would beat Dem's score of dead townspeople. He was heading the charge and ready to go into his fighting position on the horse, when the sight of two colossal beings standing at the forefront of the townspeople shook his confidence. "What the hell are these?" he asked himself. Moro, who was riding next to him, saw Jake's reaction and simply said, "the bigger they are…" in the hopes that Jake would finish the sentence, but the answer came from Dem as he rode past them at full speed screaming, "THE HARDER THEY FALL." Dem's horse thundered forward while Jake and Moro kept their speed to preserve stamina. As Dem got close to the two figures, the woman leapt into the air flying towards him at a blinding speed, she twitched in the air and landed gently on her feet. Dem's horse ran past Sam with the headless body on it. The head rolled in afterwards and stopped inches from Sam's right foot.

Seeing Dem's quick demise, Jake and Moro slowed down their charge with the objective of stopping and talking to these warriors, but the raiders behind them did not see their tactics and kept the charge. As the raiders drew closer, Sam leapt to meet them with his axe moving at a blurring speed. He ran into their midst and spun around at extreme speed sending half of the raiders to their maker in a matter of seconds. Jemma joined the fight with her sword slashing right and left. In a matter of minutes, the raiders were all dead and Jake and Moro sat there on their horses dumbfounded. The crowd behind Sam and Jemma also stood silently with the majority having their mouths open in awe. Then Jake and Moro got off their horses and walked over to Sam and Jemma who were covered in the raiders blood but had not even broken a sweat.

"Good day to you mighty warriors," said Moro as he looked at the raiders in pieces on the ground. Jake just stared blankly at the fighting duo thinking they must be demons. As the threat was gone, both weapons vanished from Sam and Jemma's hands making Jake truly believe his theory. "Good day," said Sam, snatching Jake from his own mind.

Moro then walked over to Jemma and said, "You have done this town and us a great service. These raiders were threatening to kill us if we did not raid with them and now you have freed us from their talons. We thank you, milady." Jake was very surprised at Moro's quick thinking and took a step closer to him nodding in approval to what he said.

Jemma laughed at their faces and said, "Do you really think we are that stupid to believe your clear lie? We saw you leading the charge!" Then Moro slowly pulled out a tail-lace from his pocket and showed it to Jemma. It had an engraving of a bear on it, signifying that this belonged to a senior officer of the bear tribe, the tribe of Jemma's ancestors. When Sam saw the tail-lace, he had a memory flash. He was in a large hall and there was a crest of a bear above the door. Sam was a child at the time and heard his mother say to him, "Get your sister and come eat, it's bad enough we came from bears, we don't need to act like them." As quickly as the memory came, it left. Sam had a million questions but the one that really stood out was, "I have a sister?"

"SAM," hearing Jemma call his name loudly jolted him into the current situation, "What do you think?"

Sam looked at both Jake and Moro and then back at Jemma. "I doubt they will be much trouble now. I see no need to kill them." Jemma nodded and started walking slowly towards the inn. Sam followed her and then both Jake and Moro trailed behind.

Out of Sam and Jemma's earshot, Jake asked Moro. "Why did you show them my tail-lace and how do you even have it?"

Moro simply smiled and said, "I told you it will save our lives one day, but nooo, you wanted to throw it and your past behind. You should listen to me more often, Jake." With that, they opened the inn door and walked inside.

Chapter 2
Origins

Sam was playing with his favorite toy outside their house while his father and mother were working in the garden. It was a warm spring day and Sam was wearing a red tunic with his favorite green leggings.

His mother, a tall blue-eyed woman was pruning the Papaya tree. Sam was hoping he would be as tall as she was since she did not need a ladder to reach the high branches. She was a strong woman from the highlands and was respected for her wisdom and power. He heard her whispering "kizzeb" under her breath when a thorn from the rose bush dug into her leg. This was her swear word. Sam did not know what it meant, but knew it was bad. His father was building a small bed which Sam thought was for him. But then the father turned to the mother and asked, "Will this hold her enough till she turns four?" Sam was wondering who they were talking about as he clearly was a boy.

A group of riders showed up on large black horses that had red eyes and breathed smoke. They jumped off their horses and ran straight at Sam's parents. With a flash, the first two of the riders were dead, with blood spewing from their decapitated bodies. Sam's mother had a sickle in her

19

hand which appeared from nowhere and dripped blood as she towered over the two dead bodies. His father had already dispatched the other two with the sword that appeared in his hand. But then an arrow whooshed by Sam's ear and got his mother in the heart. She slumped to the ground instantly. His father, a highlander himself, jumped to her side but the second arrow found its mark in his heart.

A dark-faced person then came for Sam. Sam heard a baby cry but did not know the source as he was paralyzed with fear. The attackers turned their attention to where the sound came from, giving Sam the split-second window to find his courage and run. A searing pain shot through the five-year-old's right thigh.

Sam woke up with a startle and felt the scar on his right thigh. *Is this a memory?* he thought to himself. *Is this how I got this scar?*

He got up from his bed in the inn and looked out of the window. His room was on the first floor of the two-story structure and overlooked a green valley, while Jemma's room was opposite his and overlooked the desert. They both seemed content with their views. As he looked onto the orange land during the shafaq, Sam tried to remember more of his dream, but it started slipping away the minute he opened his eyes. Feeling that there was nothing better to do, he washed his face in the basin in the room, put on his tunic and the new leggings he had acquired from the raiders and went downstairs for breakfast.

As he walked into the dining hall of the inn, Sam noticed that Jemma was already there, eating her breakfast. She was eating scrambled eggs with cheese and bacon on the side.

Being the only person there, he joined her at the table. There was little conversation at first, but then Jemma suddenly laughed. Sam looked at her puzzled and she exclaimed, "My father never let me have bacon, and as an adult, I now have it every day. I feel I am being rebellious." Having no memory of his parents, beyond what he saw in his dream, Sam did not see the humor in her statement and turned back to his oatmeal that had just been delivered by Lya.

"I have a memory of a house and garden," Sam said suddenly, "this means I grew up in Kiaff, as Vegna is mostly desert."

Jemma looked at him and considered his words for a second and said, "Seems like a fair analysis, shall we consider going to Kiaff then? To help you find your memories?"

Sam did not understand why she wanted to be part of this, after all, less than a week ago their paths had never crossed. "Sure," he said, with his customary emotionless demeanor.

Jake and Moro then showed up and joined the duo for breakfast.

"What's our next move?" Moro asked with a smile on his face. Jake again nodded in approval keeping his words to himself.

Sensing that the two raiders wanted to stay with them, Jemma thought they could help on their journey, so she said, "Sam needs help with some memories, and we plan to go to Kiaff to hunt some down."

As Moro was about to give his feedback, Jake jumped in saying, "Mind if we tag along?"

Sam turned to Jake with an emotionless face and said, "Sure."

By noon, both suns were well into the sky and Sam, Jemma, Moro and Jake were getting ready to leave. Lya walked over to Jake and handed him a small bundle. "It's not much, but it will keep you fed for part of the trip," she said.

Jake opened the bundle to reveal some bread, dried meat, spices and a block of cheese. "Thank you, but Kiaff is only a couple of days' ride from here, this is too much," he said.

"Even though Sanctuary is between both kingdoms, it is still considered far from both. And if you make a detour, you will not go hungry," she answered. With that, the riders mounted their steeds and rode off.

By the first sunset, the scenery had changed to be filled with lush forests, large trees, thick undergrowth and loads of small animals darting along the path of the four riders. The horses were starting to get tired, and the travelers decided to set up camp for the night. Within a few minutes, they had a fire going and used some of Lya's food to make a fireplace stew. Moro had gone to find some firewood while Jake overlooked the cooking. Sam and Jemma sat in silence listening to the fire crackling and the swishing sounds of the animals traveling around them at super speed. Then night set in, and the animals slowed down and started making their way to their burrows. Jemma was setting up her sleeping bag when a rabbit suddenly appeared by her side. It had just lost its speed and was trying to get into its burrow which was now blocked by Jemma's sleeping bag. It piqued her interest that the rabbit was purple, but not seeing many rabbits in her life, she was not sure if this was a special bunny. Feeling sorry for the little creature, she moved her sleeping bag a few meters away, letting the animal in, and she grabbed a few leaves and pushed them into the hole behind the rabbit for a snack if it got hungry in the night. Then Jemma whispered into the rabbit's hole "night night," and laid her head to sleep.

Jemma walked along the edge of the pool in her garden, her curly hair blowing in the autumn breeze. She could feel a chill in the air but was too stubborn to listen to her nanny to 'put something on.' She heard the nanny complain to her father about it. "This girl of yours is gonna be the death of me." She would hear her say. The father would always tell the nanny the same answer, "She is her parent's daughter," and laugh. Jemma didn't have friends, so she would befriend animals and insects and today was special because a frog found its way to her garden. Jemma was so happy hopping around with the frog until her father came and saw that. "This is a disgusting frog, and you are happy keeping its company?" he said.

"But it's my fwend," she answered in her little voice. "Why can't I play with the other kids I see outside our home?" she asked feeling terribly sad.

"You are too young to play with these kids. Now stop asking me silly questions and get ready for dinner." Her father said and turned and walked away.

"Not fair," Jemma said, and tears swelled up in her eyes.

A rustling near her head woke Jemma up from her memory with a startle. She looked around and there was the purple rabbit sitting there staring at her. She felt the rabbit's mind touch hers and with a short flash of images, understood that the rabbit was grateful for her act as others of her species did not have kindness in them, and she was sure the rabbit promised her safety in the forest whenever she was there. She stared back for a second and then the bunny hopped back into its hovel. Feeling that dawn was upon them, she decided it's not worth going back to sleep and got up and stretched her lean body driving away the stiffness of the night. She packed her sleeping bag and walked over to where the horses were tethered and strapped the sleeping bag back on her horse. She heard a movement in the undergrowth and peered to see if anyone or anything was attacking them, but there was no movement. So, she fanned the fire and started boiling water for coffee.

By the time shafaq was over, and the second sun found its way to the sky, the travelers had been on the road for over two hours, they rode in silence while the forest animals were zipping and zapping around them like bullets. Suddenly, all four horses stood still. In the distance, trees were being leveled by some giant creature. It was heading for them and was moving fast. Before they could figure out what it was, a giant bear appeared in front of them. The bear stood on his hind legs and roared loudly, making the already skittish horses tremble with fear. As Sam and Jemma were getting ready to summon their weapons, a purple blur passed the travelers and went straight through the bear, making a rabbit sized hole in its torso. The Bear made no sound but simply slumped to the side. The blur then came towards them and stopped a few meters from Jemma. The rabbit stood still for one second before zooming by them again and disappearing into the undergrowth. Sam turned to Jemma with clear confusion on his face while Jake and Moro stared at each other with their mouths open. Without saying a word, Jemma nudged her horse and they continued on their journey to Kiaff.

The rest of the day went on without any further incidents. By nightfall, they decided to set camp again as they were only half a day's ride from the gates of Kiaff and agreed that it would be best if they get there during the day. Just like the previous night, Moro went to get the firewood, but this time, Jake went with him, and Sam and Jemma stayed by the campfire.

Once away from the fire, Jake turned to Moro and asked, "Do you think these two know something about the bear on my tail-lace? The bear insignia really changed their perspective."

Moro smiled and said, "Frankly, I don't care, Jake, but I can tell you that we are safe with them. Now that the gang is dead, we are better off being with these two than being alone to fend for ourselves or even worse, be in prison!"

Jake smiled and nodded in agreement. "But have you seen how their weapons appear from thin air?" asked Jake.

"Yeah," said Moro. "I have never seen or heard of this before, we should ask them."

Back at camp, the last of the food offered by Lya was brewing in a pot over the fire and the scent was tantalizing. This time Jemma was cooking, and she added some herbs she had freshly picked up and all four were drooling over the food waiting for it to be ready. Jake could no longer hold his curiosity and asked, "How do you make weapons appear from thin air?"

Jemma was the first to answer, "I am not sure, there is a story my father told me once about a tribe that was given a gift by the old gods to defend themselves. All they had to do was will a weapon for defending themselves or the oppressed and a weapon appear in their right hand. All descendants from the tribe had the gift. My father could never do it, though he did experiment on me to see if there was something special, and he said my mother had it. But she died giving birth to me, so I could not learn more from her."

Sam was taken by Jemma's story but offered little enlightenment on the subject by simply answering, "In my case, the Axe simply appears when I need to fight."

"What about the writing on them, I was not able to read it," said Moro.

"And I can read many languages," he added feeling smug. "I don't know the language, but I can read the line on my axe; it reads 'son of man, slayer of demons'," said Sam.

"Mine reads 'Daughter of Queens, slayer of men'," Jemma added.

"So, between you, neither man nor demon survives," said Jake.

"Adding the purple bunny, neither does beast." Laughed Moro. Both Moro and Jake slept deeply that night as they had been exhausted from lack of sleep for the last two days due to being worried that either Sam or Jemma might have slashed them in the night.

All four travelers woke up at the dawn of the next morning and stretched out their bodies in the orange hue of the shafaq before they started their descent from the camping grounds on the hill towards the gates of the Kiaff kingdom. The earth was wet with dew, but the horses kept a steady footing and managed to make their way down the steep sections, gracefully. By noon, they were at the gates of Kiaff and as they were about to join the hordes of merchants and travelers through the gates, Jemma leapt off her horse, landing softly on her feet and knelt down to fix her shoe when a purple blur

26

sped near her and stopped dead by her foot. She looked down to see the rabbit who saved their life the day before. She tried petting it, but like a flash of lightning, the rabbit sped off in the direction of the forests and was out of sight in an instant. "I think he was saying goodbye," said Sam.

"I think you are right," answered Jemma. Then she turned towards the forest and smiled.

Chapter 3
Kiaff

Ash and Tray really hated to be on gate guard duty, but not as much as being together on this duty. To them, being together was a joke in the making ever since the sergeant called their names without using the word 'and'. Now, they stood at the gates of Kiaff watching the hordes of people walk in while trying to identify the troublemakers.

"Since the last battle was fought only a week ago and the war has ended, it's a relief not to worry about spies anymore," said Ash, trying to raise the somber mood.

"But we are still together and on gate duty. Still a crap day if you ask me!" retorted Tray. As they looked on and tried their best scrutinizing the entrants of the city, their attention was drawn to four travelers. Two of them looked like descendants of giants and the other two like raiders. Neither of the guards wanted to talk to the large couple, but they really wanted to stop the smaller ones. "Looks like we have something here, Ash," said Tray pointing at Jake and Moro.

"Alright then," sighed Ash, "let's do our work."

"Oi, you there," called out Ash signaling to Jake and Moro, "this way."

Jake and Moro walked over to Ash and Tray followed by Sam and Jemma.

"What brings you here," asked Ash to Moro.

But Sam answered, "They are with me, helping me find something missing."

As Ash was about to answer, Tray nudged him to look at Jemma's tail-lace. Ash immediately apologized and ushered them through.

"What was that about," asked Sam to Jemma. "My tail-lace signifies that I am a high-born from the free tribes. We have not been in the war and have made sure that both sides do not come close to our lands. However, both kingdoms fear that if we join the other, we will tip the balance of war. We brokered a peace between the two kingdoms which was signed at the end of the last battle. Now our crest is welcome, respected and feared in both kingdoms."

"See, I told you it pays to be with the good guys," whispered Jake to Moro.

The travelers walked through the gates of Kiaff to see the entrance of the city. The roads were of cobblestone and wrapped around the city in a circular form. It looked like the city was designed around the great castle and circular streets and houses were built around it, making larger circles until the great castle became the center of a large Kingdom. Sam and Jemma walked ahead trying to find an inn they can stay at for the duration of their visit. They passed a few of the outer circles when they found an inn they liked. Interestingly, it was called Sanctuary. Like the town where they stayed at the last inn. As they entered, the air smelt surprisingly fresh as opposed to the usual smell of stale beer and smoke. A burly man walked towards them welcoming them.

"Greetings travelers. Welcome to Sanctuary inn. What can I offer you?" asked Paul, the inn owner.

"An ale for now and four beds for the night," answered Sam.

"Well, I have three rooms, if any of you are okay to share," answered Paul.

"We can share," said Moro pointing to himself and Jake with Jake nodding beside him.

"Then it's settled," smiled Paul.

As Paul was guiding the travelers to their rooms, he turned to Jemma and stared into her eyes with a look of bewilderment. Jemma was accustomed to men openly making advances, but Paul's stare was that of someone who was trying to remember things. Then he turned his gaze to her tail where he saw the tail-lace and took a step back looking afraid.

"Are you from the Crow tribe?" he asked her with a trembling voice.

"Yes, and what's wrong?" Jemma said.

She felt a fake relief in his tone when he answered "Oh, I, I, I thought it was the Eagle tribe for a second. Scary folks those ones." Jemma could see he was lying. Even though the Crow and Eagle tribes were not allies, she knew that the Eagle tribe were civilized and not raiders. Something was off with Paul. But she brushed off her concern and walked into the room that was set to be hers.

After a warm bath, Jemma got dressed in a clean sky-blue tunic and leather leggings with her newly shined boots which Paul had offered to do for all travelers. She left the room to meet Sam, Moro and Jake talking by Sam's door. All of them were dressed in clean fresh clothes and had shaved their beards which had grown during their journey. Sam's purple eyes shown bright, and it was the first time Jemma had noticed them. Moro had his hair shaved off but kept a goatee while Jake had shaved his beard but combed his curly black hair back. When they saw her, they walked over to her and together they all took the stairs from the second floor of the stone-built inn to the ground floor. The suns had set by then, and the inn was alive with music and people drinking and eating. They realized that the crowd looked more sophisticated than the inns they usually visit. They walked over to Paul to thank him for the new clothes. Jemma smiled at him and said, "Thank you for this tunic, it is in my favorite color."

Paul gave a big smile saying, "I was worried you would not like it. But I had a gut feeling you would like it."

After dinner, Sam and Jemma decided to go for a walk and discover the city while Jake and Moro decided to turn in early. As they walked in silence, both Sam and Jemma took in the sights. Three and four-story buildings made from rocks and clean and flat cobble stoned streets. They met a few people along the way who were quick with a "Good evening" and smile.

Then Jemma turned to Sam and said, "I have never been to this part of Kiaff, the people seem nice. Does any of this jog your memory?"

Sam shook his head and sighed a sad 'no'. Suddenly, a figure caught Sam's eye, in the darkness. The figure looked like a shadow. When Sam turned to get a better look, it darted behind a wall behind them.

Jemma saw the same thing and without saying a word, the duo walked on at a slow and steady pace. As they turned a corner, they both hid in a doorway of a house and waited to see if that person was following them. A few seconds later, the figure turned the same corner. Sam and Jemma both grabbed the man's arms at the same time. He shrieked with surprise and fear looking at both of them and his eyes darting from one to the other.

"Who are you and why are you following us?" demanded Sam.

"I am sorry, I am sorry," was all the man could say.

"Look, we will not harm you if you tell us why you are following us," said Jemma in a calm and nonthreatening tone.

"I was asked by Paul to see where you go," answered the man. "I am Fillian, Paul's stable boy," he said with his voice trembling.

"Why would Paul want us followed?" asked Sam to Jemma.

"Not sure, but he does act weird around me. I will ask him tonight when we return," she answered.

"What about him?" Sam said, pulling Fillian towards him.

"Oh, I will go home and be with my family. I will not return to the Inn, I promise," said Fillian and tears formed in his eyes as he was convinced these two warriors will kill him.

"I believe him, let him go," said Jemma releasing her hold on Fillian's arm.

"Okay," said Sam letting go of Fillian's other arm.

Fillian fell to the ground, his legs betraying him. He started crying softly as he saw the two purple eyed giants walk away, leaving him to live. He was sure he would die there.

With nothing jogging Sam's memory, the duo decided to go back to the inn to talk to Paul. When they got there, the crowd had died out and Paul was busy cleaning up the place. They sat at the bar and waited for Paul to pour their drinks.

Sam had his Honey Ale while Jemma had a beer. As Paul was serving them, he kept looking into Jemma's eyes.

Jemma then calmly asked Paul, "Why did you send someone to follow us?"

Paul looked shocked, embarrassed and terrified in one go. "I-I-I look after all my clients," he said.

"Are you really that stupid?" asked Sam, "Do you really think this is an actual answer?"

With that, Sam's temper had heated immediately at the insult to his intellect and grabbed Paul from behind the Bar and threw him into the tables behind them. Paul immediately broke into tears and started crying, "Please, please, I will tell you everything, but don't hurt me, I beg you."

Sam and Jemma both looked at Paul and said together, "Speak."

"About twenty years ago, I had just opened this inn. Business had not started yet and I was desperate, so I would let anyone in to stay, no matter how shady they were. This attracted the wrong crowd, as opposed to what you see today. My business was frequented by low lives of the outer circles of the Kingdom, the thieves, cut-throats, pickpockets and the rest of their nasty friends and business partners," Paul started. "One day, a well-dressed man showed up, he looked rich and powerful. That said, he did have distinguishing features, a scar on the left side of his face. It cut from the top left of his temple down through the eye and ended by the right side of his mouth. His eye was intact, but it was a different color than the other, one was green and the other blue."

Jemma cut him, asking, "Did he tell you his name?" Her tone being angry and curious at the same time.

"Not at first," answered Paul, "but hear me out."

"I offered the man a room for the night, and he booked it for a few days, and then booked five other rooms for the same period. A day later, four men and a woman showed up. They looked like warriors and all of them had a tail-lace like yours," he said pointing to Jemma's tail. "The next morning, all six of them rode away, but two days later the gentleman and lady returned with a baby wrapped in a sky-blue blanket. She had purple eyes. When I asked them for their names, they said they were Eli and Ella which sounded like an open lie. The next morning, they rode away but not before giving me a generous sum of money and threatening to find and kill me if I ever told anyone of this. Which I have not until today." Paul stopped talking and drank from the goblet that was in front of him. "When I saw you earlier today, with your purple eyes and tail-lace I guessed that you might be the baby and you wanted to cut the loose ends in your story." Paul went for the goblet again and realized it was not his to start with and put it back with a little sign of disgust on his face.

Jemma's head was reeling. This man described her father in detail. But who was the woman? So, she asked Paul to describe the woman. "She was a tall lady but always carried a bow and arrow with her. She was rather pleasant and patient and when they arrived, she stood at the door and watched children play. She had red hair and…"

"Green eyes…" interrupted Jemma.

"YES!" exclaimed Paul as if he was pleased she knew who he was talking about.

Sam was listening to this story wondering how this is related to Jemma, but her face showed no emotion. Inside, she was furious, but on the outside, nothing showed. When Paul was done, she got up and went to her room. Sam sat with Paul for a while trying to get any other information from him; however, that proved to be a futile exercise. Sam bid Paul good night and walked up to his room. As he passed Jemma's room, he heard a sniffle from within. He tapped lightly at the door and Jemma opened it with red eyes and nose, he could tell she was crying, and did not want to embarrass her, but she just walked into him, hugged him and sobbed. Sam said nothing but stood there holding a broken-hearted Jemma who had just discovered her life was a lie.

All these years of experimentation by her father onto how to call the weapon from thin air was not for love or interest, he had kidnapped her from her family and tried to learn the secret. To which there was no answer but a blessing from the old gods. She remembered how she had to work extra hard to get his approval, everything she did was for him, and now, to discover that all her life was a lie, was too much for her to bear that day. Her sobs slowly faded, and Sam felt she was falling asleep, so he carried her to her bed, laid her there and went on to his room. In his room, Sam stared out of the window at the stone city and thought of the forests beyond, a place where the evil of man did not reach. He sighed lightly and lay in his bed to sleep.

Morning came quickly for Sam, he felt he had just fallen asleep. He got up, washed his face and walked downstairs for breakfast. Jemma was already there, eating her eggs and bacon. He joined her at the table and said nothing. She looked at him with her usual demeanor and smiled dryly. "Some story this guy told us," she said, "looks like I am not my father's daughter after all."

Sam looked at her silently for a second and then said, "We came to find my memories and ended up finding yours. Since mine looks like a dead end, why not follow your path for a while. That said, I do not understand how you ended up by the river in Sanctuary when the free tribes are in the other direction from here." Jemma took a deep breath and told Sam how she had just finished her mission of finding and killing her father's killer in Vegna. The assassin was sent to the free tribes to kill their leader and try to blame it on Kiaff, but the free tribes saw through the ruse and elected her to execute justice. But before he died, her father had told her that the truth she seeks is in Vegna, but she had thought he was delirious.

"Now, it's a different story," she said.

"As there is nothing for me here, why not go to Vegna and try to find my memories and that truth your father spoke of?" Sam said. Jemma nodded in agreement.

Jake and Moro joined them for breakfast asking if they found any clues in the night. "We found interesting information that leads us to Vegna. We think we should take our search there," said Sam.

Jemma just looked at Sam as he suggested they pack and take their search to the other kingdom.

"Sounds like a plan to me," said Jake, "I really do miss the Vegnan wine," he added with a smile.

Moro looked concerned and turned to Jake saying, "But we are known there, we might get into trouble with our debts."

Jemma turned to them saying, "Don't stress that, we will be with you and through my diplomatic relationship with them, we will resolve your issues." Two hours later, the travelers were on their way through the gates of Kiaff towards Vegna.

Chapter 4
The Secret of Speed

It was late afternoon and the first sun had set. But the animals still whizzed by Blandi constantly. Ever since he lost his eyes, his sense of hearing became acute, and he could tell which animal moved and where they were. Blandi sat in silence by a brook in the forest when he heard hoofbeats of four horses. From the sound of the hoofs, he could tell they were four travelers, three men and a woman. As the travelers approached, Blandi could hear their breathing and heartbeats, he could tell they had just left Kiaff to Vegna as if on a mission. "Hello there," he said with his old voice, "welcome weary travelers."

Moro and Jake got off their horses and walked towards the old man. "Slow down you two," he said, "there is a squirrel passing by," and a second later, a blur passed right in front of the duo who stood there dumbfounded.

"How did you know that, old man?" asked Jake.

"Easy, my boy, I am old and blind, but I see more than you young fellows. I was there when animals got to be fast and will be there when they slow down again."

This subject was always an interesting topic for Jake, he really wanted to understand how certain animals went fast while others did not change with the second sun.

"So, you know how this happened?" exclaimed Jake excitedly.

"I was there when it happened," answered Blandi. "Do you want to receive this knowledge?"

"Yes, of course!" exclaimed Jake.

"Well," said Blandi. "Have a seat!" Gesturing for Jake to sit next to him on the large rock.

Blandi started, "Millennia ago, we and the animals were no different, we all had the same speed and strength. And, WE didn't have tails. We belonged to a species they called *Human* at the time. And these ancestors of ours had made great advances in mechanics and a thing they called science, which was a study of everything."

"Everything?" exclaimed Jake, "Who studies everything?"

"Listen," said Blandi, "for there is more. So, these humans started learning about all the secrets of the world we live in. They had created large structures, and things so small, we would not be able to see. And then they discovered something called *genes*. Apparently, these are things in each of us which determine our features and characteristics. One day, the leading scientists started playing with the genes of living creatures. Their first subjects were small forest animals. Oh, the horrors they did to them…"

Blandi then took a deep breath and asked Moro to fetch him some water from the brook as he was getting thirsty. Moro went to the brook and filled Blandi's goatskin with water and returned. After drinking his fill, Blandi continued.

"So, the scientists did all these experiments and tests on these small animals trying to change them. Most of these animals died as a result of all this genetic experimentation which went on for years and years. However, a war broke out between the many kingdoms of the time. With all their advancements and ability to build, these humans had created weapons that could destroy everything, even the fabric of life itself. And they unleashed these weapons on each other in the big war. All what they had built was destroyed in a matter of hours. And all the secret genetic research turned into vapor and became part of the air we breathe. This changed everything on this planet. Our trees changed, our senses changed, and our appearances changed, hence the tails we have now. In those days, these tails did not exist outside the body.

"And when the new sun appeared in the sky, most of the forest animals got superspeed and super strength. At first, no one understood what was happening and many were killed in the pursuit of understanding this new phenomenon. Animals would even go so fast that even squirrels started knocking down the trees they live in. But when only one sun was in the sky, what we know as shafaq, the animals became dizzy and tired, making themselves easy prey to all who hunt them. It turned out that the first sun is the sun we always had, and the second sun is the new sun which activates these special genes in these small animals. So, the horses, us, the bears, lions and cattle do not get the speed, but we did get tails."

Jake was dumbfounded, "Humans you say? And scientists? And experiments? You must think we are really stupid. It was the old gods that gave these animals these powers and shaped us in their image…with a tail!" he snapped at Blandi.

39

Blandi smiled and said, "That may be true, but there is no way you can prove it."

Jake, feeling frustrated at Blandi's ridiculous story shouted back, "Neither can you, now, can you?"

Blandi smiled and simply said, "No." After hearing this long-winded story, Sam and Jemma decided that they have lost enough time to superstition and needed to be on their way. Vegna was three days' ride away and they needed answers. So, they wished Blandi the best and went on their way. Moro, being too captivated by the old man's knowledge, decided to stay with him and learn more about the world he lives in. Also, he did not want to go to Vegna as he was sure he will either face death or prison there. Jake on the other hand, was keen to go Vegna as he was not wanted there and had people and places he wanted to visit. After their final farewells, Sam, Jemma and Jake started their journey to Vegna.

By sundown, the trio who had been traveling silently found a clearing for a camping spot. Jake started the fire and Sam went to find wood while Jemma fished in the saddles for the ingredients for dinner. Sam returned with enough firewood for the whole night to see Jake and Jemma sitting on opposite sides of the fire silently. Within minutes, the aroma of the food filled the air. Jake then broke the silence saying, "Strange about Moro wanting to stay back. I thought he would stick with us."

"I thought you would have stayed with him," retorted Jemma, "you seemed like old friends."

Jake lowered his gaze and softly answered, "We knew each other, but not for long, we just stuck with each other when we joined the raiders, we always felt like outcasts, and Moro doesn't really know my real name." Both Jemma and

Sam stared at him while he took a deep breath and raised his head slowly saying, "Kahl."

"But why would you hide your name?" asked Sam.

"It is clearly a name from the warrior tribe that was wiped out in the past," said Jake. "My father was a descendant of this tribe and kept the name in the family in the hopes someone would find me. Sadly, both my parents died to the fever while I was young, and our neighbors took me in and called me Jake to keep my identity a secret and to keep me safe."

"Today is one hell of a day of revelations," said Sam sarcastically as he got up to add wood to the fire. "Seems we learn new things all the time."

Jemma turned to Kahl and said, "To keep your identity safe, we will continue to call you Jake. But thank you for being honest with us."

"On the subject of being honest..." Jake pulled out the tail-lace Moro had shown them previously and said, "this was my father's, it is not Moro's, it's mine, but Moro kept it in case anyone searched me."

Upon seeing the tail-lace with the bear insignia on it, Sam remembered his vision of being in the hall and the bear crest above the entrance. He told Jemma and Jake about the vision and hearing his mother telling him to call his sister. When Sam was done sharing his memory, Jake looked him straight in the eye and told him he knew of the hall Sam had mentioned and he knew where it was. He promised Sam he will take him to see it in Vegna where they were heading to find out more about Jemma's origins.

On the second day, as the trio rode silently towards Sanctuary to restock on their way to Vegna, a purple blur passed by Jemma's horse and stopped a few meters ahead for a split second before darting off again.

"The rabbit!" exclaimed Jemma happily, then turned to Sam and said, "He is my friend!" with a bright smile on her face. A few minutes later, they heard a loud roar in the distance, which seemed to be cut short as if interrupted. The trio kept their pace, but Sam and Jemma had the hands ready to summon the weapons. As they rounded the bend in the road, a purple blur whizzed by, stopped long enough for them to realize it's the purple rabbit, but he had blood on him, and then he took off again…so fast that the blood fell off him. A few minutes later, they saw a bear slumped on the side of the road with a bunny sized hole in his torso.

"Do you think this bunny is a bear hunter?" Sam asked, turning to Jemma as they passed the lifeless body of the bear.

"I don't know, but I would like to think he is watching out for me," came her reply. Jake, who was riding behind them was simply astonished by how the universe conspires to look after these two and wondered if being with them was also part of the universe's plan.

The trio rode on for a while longer and then decided to stop for lunch. They found a good resting spot by a brook and dismounted from their horses. The horses drank from the brook and so did their riders. As Jake was raising his head from the water, an arrow passed right in front of him. As if it was intended for his head, but he had moved suddenly. He took a step back as the second arrow hissed by him and got half buried in the tree beside him. "We are under attack!" he screamed as he ran to hide behind a tree. Sam and Jemma had already noticed the attack and summoned their weapons. Being an accomplished marksman, Jake ran to his horse and pulled out his bow and arrow in the knowledge that he can down the attackers from a safe distance. A couple of arrows missed him along the way. When he found his weapon, Jake notched the first arrow, drew and released. A muffled cry came out of the bush in the distance. Jake's second arrow also found its mark in the heart of one of their attackers. Then five men rushed towards the trio. Two were holding axes, two were holding long swords and the fifth one had a club. Sam stood still as one axe-man and one swordsman approached him. As the assailant's sword swished towards Sam, it was met by a blue axe which shattered the sword to bits and continued to separate the axe-man's torso from his legs. Sam then took a step forward with his elbow raised, driving it into the swordsman's neck—snapping it instantly.

Jemma ran towards her assailants at a blinding speed with a red light in her hand. With one smooth move, both attackers near her slumped down, lifeless. Jake, however, was having a hard time with the bandit with the club, who was pounding at Jake, but all Jake had was his bow which he used to defend himself. The bandit pounded Jake relentlessly until the bow broke. The bandit raised his club to deliver the final blow, then he just stood there, his eyes rolled back and he fell to the side. Jake saw Sam standing behind the attacker and the blue axe shimmering out of sight. Without warning, an arrow flew past Sam's ear and thudded in the tree behind Jake.

"With no long-range weapons, we are dead," whispered Jake.

"Not yet," said Sam as he turned to join Jemma on her run towards the location where the arrows came from. As they got there, three bandits were waiting: two with swords and one with a bow and arrow. Sam took the bandit on the right while

Jemma took the bandit on the left. The fight lasted mere seconds and ended with two dead bandits. The third bandit was notching his arrow aiming it at Sam when a green light passed through the bushes and hit the bandit so hard, it knocked him off his feet. Sam and Jemma looked on as the glowing green arrow then simply shimmered out of sight. They turned to where Jake was and saw a green bow in his hand. The bow was similar in style to their magical weapons. It was made of green light and a black line ran through the handle with an inscription similar to what the other two had, which read: "swift death, from afar". They barely had time to see it as it shimmered away in Jake's hand that had now started trembling as he had no clue what just happened.

"What the hell was that?" asked Jake with a very shaky voice. "What just happened…" he continued with his voice moving between fear and excitement. He started thrusting his hands trying to get the bow to reappear, but nothing happened. He tried again and again in vain.

"It might be that your gift finally appeared," said Sam, "you know, being of the tribe that got the gift from the gods," he continued.

"But this has never happened to me before. As the story goes, this should happen all the time!" said Jake still trying to get the bow to appear.

"Mine only appears when my intention is true," said Jemma.

"Mine too," said Sam.

"But I spent my whole life raiding and fighting, and this never happened to me. And I did intend to raid at the time!" said Jake, "Why did it not show up then?"

"Maybe it was for the wrong cause." said Jemma, "When fighting for a good reason, these weapons appear, but for the wrong cause, they do not assist you. We might find out more as we travel, but for now, we and the horses are watered, and I would like to put some space between us and here before nightfall."

The other two nodded in agreement and moved towards their horses. Then Jake turned and walked to the dead bodies, checked them for what coins they had and returned a moment later, smiling at Sam and Jemma who were already mounted on their steeds. "We will stay in the best inns in Vegna," he said with a big smile on his face waving a bulging coin bag.

Chapter 5
Sanctuary

Lya was practicing her new song which was giving her a hard time. The beginning of it was too low and fast but the middle really showed off her talents. She was trying to sing it with tune, but it came out as a quick succession of words as opposed to the melodious tune she had in mind. She started and stopped herself a few times until she got her song right:

For what does it give me
When I have my man
And he doesn't listen?
For what does it mean
When there's snow on the land
But it doesn't glisten?
Iiiiiiiiiiiiiiii
Need to be heaaaaaaaaard
Myyyyyyyyyyy
Lesson is leaaaarnt
A listener is who my man will beeeeeee…

Lya jumped when she heard a clap in the tavern and turned to see Ben there in the shadows.

"What are you doing here? You gave me a fright!" she shouted at him holding her heart.

"Listening to your golden voice, my dear. It's tantalizing."

"Off with you. You lying oaf!" she snapped. "It's bad enough I caught you cheating, now you think your sweet words will change how I think? Begone!"

"But honey, you know I love you," Ben said with a pleading voice, "just give me another chance."

"You had your chance," she said, "now it's gone. Leave me be and stay away from me."

The door of the tavern opened and in walked three figures. Two silhouettes were familiar but a third was relatively new. Ben grabbed his recently healed hand and rubbed the scar as he saw Jemma walk through, followed by Sam and the raider. Lya welcomed the interruption and walked over to them with a big smile on her face.

"Welcome back Sam and Jemma, glad to see you again," she said with a smile, but then her expression changed when she saw Jake. "But why is he still with you?" she said, pointing at Jake.

"He has mended his ways, Lya," said Jemma with no explanation beyond that.

"I am sorry for all the trouble I caused, Ma'am," said Jake as he walked over to Lya, with a small coin pouch in his hand. "This is what I had taken from you, it is rightfully yours, and now I return it."

As he got closer, he had a good look at Lya's face, noticing her bright eyes, black hair and beautiful features, he was struck by her beauty. With him so close, Lya saw the man behind the bandit and his chiseled jaw and wide shoulders, she also saw kindness in his eyes. She snatched the pouch and turned away, then she stopped, turned back and with a smile and said, "Thank you." Jake's face lit up with a massive smile.

"So, what brings you here?" asked Lya, "Did you find your memories?" she said, looking at Sam.

"Not yet, but we did find interesting info on Jemma," he said.

"So, we are now on our way to Vegna for further investigation," piped Jake smiling at Lya. Ben saw that Jake was taken by Lya and his jealousy rose. He reminded himself that he lost Lya when she caught him cheating, but he could not control his actions. Ben walked out of the shadows and stood by Lya facing Jake, and said, "So you think you can *buy* her emotions?"

Jake was immediately embarrassed by such a translation of his actions and took a step back raising his hands in front of him as if to hold down Ben's rage and explained, "No sir, not at all, I was returning what was hers, not buying anything!"

Lya, obviously bothered by Ben, pushed him to the side saying, "You have no right or say in the matter, Ben, you and I are finished, so go to your whore and leave me alone."

Jake, seeing that Lya was pushing Ben away, felt honor-bound to defend this beauty, and stood straight opposite Ben and with an angry tone said, "If you have no say in the matter, why do you have anything to say? Or do you make it your business to meddle? I suggest you leave before this situation turns ugly."

Sam, who was watching this with amusement, had had enough of this and walked over to the two men; putting his massive hands on both their shoulders, said, "Let's let the lady decide, it is clear you both are thinking of *her* best interest."

Jemma laughed out loud as did Lya, which angered Jake and Ben further. Being a hot head and sure of himself, Ben took a swing at Jake and missed. Jake then served Ben with an uppercut, sending him off his feet and onto a table behind him that buckled under his weight and crashed to the floor, making Lya shriek. Ben got up to attack Jake only to be met with Sam's large fist in his face…making the world go dark.

"Why did you punch him?" asked Jemma. "You should have let them fight it out."

"No, he did well," said Lya walking over to Jake, "some men avoid a fight and are gentle," she said smiling at him.

"Now help me move this idiot out of my establishment as he has ruined enough of my day!" With that, Sam and Jake carried Ben outside the tavern and placed him on a bench on the porch. When they returned, there were two ale's waiting for them with some food at the table where Jemma was sitting. As they sat, Lya joined them. "So, going to Halshalnd, eh? Seems like a long trip ahead of you," Lya said as she cut a piece of cheese and put it in her mouth.

"Not really, it's only a three-day ride," said Sam, wondering why she would say that.

"I have family there and have been meaning to visit, but the time was never right," said Lya looking at Jake. Realizing the hint, Jemma joined the discussion, "Why don't you come with us? Your food and voice will be welcomed on such a long and tedious journey." Lya smiled a "yes". Jake smiled, "great" and Sam was completely confused to what they were talking about. With that, he got up saying, "Thank you for the food, but I am off for a bath and a good night's sleep. Same rooms?"

Lya nodded and Sam just walked away. Jemma then dusted her hand, downed her wine and got up to leave saying, "Sam had a good idea, bath and sleep. Good night." and she walked away leaving a smiling Lya and Jake staring at each other.

Jemma was playing in the garden when her father walked out. "Show me your hands," he said as he grabbed her right hand and started feeling it. "Try to summon a weapon," he ordered, and 10-year-old Jemma started focusing on her hand hoping to please her daddy. The air around her hand shimmered and stopped. "Again," he barked, and she tried again.

"What a shame," he said with a very disappointed voice and walked away. Jemma's mood had changed completely and was feeling miserable. After he left, she kept trying to summon a weapon but all she got was a shimmer. Then the masked man came for her, he drew his dagger and ran towards her. She was terrified, but she felt a handle in her hand and acting only on instinct, swung at the assailant, chopping off his hand. She looked down at her hand and saw a ruby-like sword. The attacker was screaming in pain and her nanny ran into the garden to see what happened. Her father came out to see Jemma with the sword and smiled. The assailant cried to her father saying, "You told me she was not one of them and to dispatch her, now she took my hand!" Jemma's father just shouted orders for the staff to take him to the healer and walked away.

Jemma opened her eyes from this dream to an orange hue in her room. "Shafaq," she whispered to herself and got out of bed to wash her face. This memory bothered her throughout her life. Her father had sent this man to kill her, and if it wasn't for the sword, she would have been dead. But being a man of extreme convincing skills, he managed to get her to buy into his intentions of helping her find her weapon. She stood in the room and stared out of the window into the desert beyond which was Vegna. She turned to the basin in the room, washed her face, got dressed and went downstairs to the tavern to have breakfast. The smell of pine had started bothering her, but not enough to say anything yet. Jemma got to the tavern to see Lya and Jake still sitting at the table and in deep discussion.

"Did you even go to sleep?" she asked.

Both looked at her surprised and then to each other, "Is it morning already?" asked Jake. "I hadn't noticed!"

Lya's cheeks blushed as she smiled at Jemma and got up to clear the table. "Eggs and bacon?" she asked Jemma who nodded in response. Jake got up and went to his room without saying a word. A few minutes later, Lya returned with Jemma's breakfast who was now accompanied by Sam. "Good morning, Lya, can I have the same please?" asked Sam. Lya smiled at Sam and said, "Sure," in the way he said it. He smiled. When Lya returned with Sam's breakfast, she sat with them and re-iterated her desire to go with them to Vegna to visit her relatives. Their company would be far better than going alone she explained, and their fighting skills made it a safer trip for her. Both agreed that she was welcome, and they planned to leave Sanctuary the next morning, after some supplies were bought and Lya and Jake got some rest.

While Jake and Lya slept for the day, Sam and Jemma decided to go on a stroll in Sanctuary and see if they could learn anything new about Sam's origins. They walked around the town, passed by the merchants who displayed food, cheese, cloth, jewelry and other odds and ends. One of them stopped Jemma...offering her a pair of earrings which once she looked them over, she decided they were of no interest to her. A beggar came by them asking for coin but was sent away disappointed. A sweet smell of roasted meat filled the air, making both Sam and Jemma suddenly very hungry. They followed the scent to a small restaurant that had a few tables and even fewer patrons. The owner, a plump and jolly old man welcomed them with a smile, ushering them to a table. As they sat down, he immediately delivered two goblets of ale bearing in mind neither ordered any. They knew why this place has less patrons, the owner scams passers-by with what looks like hospitality, but in reality, charges them for things they did not order. That said, as they were both hungry, they did not complain. A few minutes later the waiter came by and took their order, which didn't take long to arrive. The food was good, but the ale felt watered down. When the food was done, Sam and Jemma got up to leave when the plump man walked over to them asking if everything was to their liking. They said, "yes," thanked him and were starting to walk away when he grabbed Sam's hand and said, "I am glad you made it," with a smile. Sam turned to him asking, "Made it?"

"Yes," said the plump man, "you ate here before battle day and told me you hope to end this war and secure peace without dying, you hoped you'd make it."

"Was I with anyone?" asked Sam.

"No, you were alone," said the man. "I even remember you telling me that there are no winning sides in a war, and you were not on either side. You had just come from Vegna and had a plan to end the battle before it starts. When I heard of the battle, I thought you died, but seeing you now gives me joy." With that the man turned away to usher new patrons into the restaurant and went off to fetch them some unrequested ale. Sam and Jemma stood there for a few minutes, then walked away with Sam saying, "So, I didn't have a side after all! Interesting."

Back at the Inn, Sam and Jemma joined Lya and Jake at the bar to share the updates with them. "It seems we are going to the right place after all," said Jake. Lya put her hand on Jake's on the bar and sounded giddy saying, "I can't wait for tomorrow to come!" Both Sam and Jemma looked at Lya who then recomposed herself and with a smile said, "Jake promised to show me the best places in Vegna, restaurants, markets and the famed Vegna winery," her face got serious for second when she continued, "where I plan to place my next order." She ended with a smile.

"Jake seems to know his way around there," said Sam. "He knows a place I have seen in my dreams, which might give us insight to my memory."

"Yeah, I had been there as a kid with my dad," said Jake. "He had said that they used to go there every year in winter." Jemma sat listening, thinking of what she would do once they get there, and she gets a minute to herself. Thinking of her diplomatic connection and wondering if she would be able to help them with their quests. Her thoughts and absent-minded smile were interrupted by the sound of a goblet being placed on the bar in front of her.

"Drink up." She heard Lya say.

Chapter 6
The Road to Vegna

The Journey began at the start of shafaq when the world resonated in orange and purple, making everything more beautiful and colorful. Sam and Jemma rode in front while Lya and Jake rode behind them. Jake and Lya were talking up a storm. She was telling him how she grew up in Sanctuary with her older brother who was an important council member and had recently wed a lady of noble descent in Kiaff and only moved there a few days prior to them arriving. She told him about Ben who she was about to marry until she caught him cheating on her with the baker's daughter. "I had just about given up on men when you walked through the door." Jake then told her all about his life in Vegna and the many jobs he had before joining the raiders. How he started off as a waiter at an inn and then was kicked out for eating the food, and then worked at the Blacksmith and was kicked out for blunting sharpened swords and eventually of his heartbreak by Melinda a few years ago when she married his best friend. Jake said that after he was forced to join the raiders due to a debt he owed the leader, he had had hoped that he would find Melinda and her husband and kill them. But after a while, he lost interest in love until he met Lya. All this discussion was going on while Sam and Jemma rode in silence. Then Lya asked, "I see you two are a perfect match for each other, what's stopping you?" Both Sam and Jemma looked at each other and laughed heartily. Lya was surprised and a bit confused by that reaction.

Jake then turned to Lya and said, "I don't think these two have hearts!"

"I heard that," Sam answered, "and we do have hearts. However, we do not have any such feelings towards each other."

"That is correct, so no assumptions please," added Jemma.

By midday, the horses were tired and the riders needed a break. They sat by a clearing to rest themselves and the horses. A purple blur zoomed through the camp and stopped at Jemma's feet. She had already collected some leaves and had them placed in front of her. "Bunny!" she exclaimed happily. The rabbit looked at her and started eating. Within a second, the food was gone but the rabbit sat still. Jemma reached out to pet him expecting him to blur out again, but the rabbit did not move. She petted his head softly and put some water near him. The rabbit looked at her, sipped the water and blurred out of the camp at super speed.

"Off to hunt bears you think?" joked Sam.

"I doubt he is hunting as much as he is protecting us," answered Jemma still smiling from petting the rabbit. Lya was watching this in a clear shock.

"Was that a purple rabbit you just petted?" she asked in awe.

"Yeah," smiled Jemma.

"They are super rare and impossible to tame," said Lya, "I heard stories of people trying to tame them who ended up being sped through and killed by them! But they say for the ones who become their friend, the rabbits become more loyal than a dog and more vicious in defending their friend. Count yourself very lucky to have this one as a friend. You will always be safe in the forest." On that note, the travelers got up and got ready to get back on the road.

After a few hours' ride, at the end of the day, Sam emerged from the forest followed by Jemma, then Lya and finally Jake. The road from now on will be through the desert. It always fascinated Lya how the forest ends in a straight line and the desert starts. It was like nature had used a ruler to divide the land between wet and dry. The traveling will be slower now as the desert sand sunk under the horses' hoofs making the steps smaller in distance and requiring more effort to travel the same distance as on hard ground. As they moved deeper into the desert, the hotter it got and the deader it seemed. No crazy fast furry creatures zooming about, no bird calls, just the sound of the wind blowing and the odd grain of sand flying into their eyes. They had been a few miles into the desert when the suns had set completely. The air grew cooler and lighter. Sam suggested resting for the night but both Jake and Jemma highlighted the importance of going on.

"At night, the temperature is low, and the horses can travel better. If we rest tonight, we will need two extra days to get to Vegna," said Jemma.

"If we travel through the night, we will come to an old structure which is now used as a resting place for travelers. We will rest during the hot days and travel in the cool evenings," explain Jake.

Seeing that he did not have any memories of such, Sam decided to trust the two and keep going. They traveled slowly and in silence with the full moon lighting up the way. The view was so serene and quiet and familiar that Sam was sure he did come from Vegna just like the restaurant owner said.

A few hours went by in silence with all four of the travelers taking in the scenery when they all saw a light flicker up ahead. "That must be the resting place," said Sam.

"But we could not have been traveling that fast!" exclaimed Jake. "The resting place should be at least a couple of hours further." Nonetheless, the travelers went on towards the light. When they got near it, they saw a large structure made of bricks and a few horses tethered outside. "That must be the place," said Lya. "But the horses will not do well in the day's heat, there must be a stable somewhere near."

As they got closer, they saw the stables and an old lady cleaning them out. "Ah," exclaimed Lya, "that must be why the horses are outside." When they had dismounted and tethered their horses, Sam led the way into the building. The wooden door creaked when he opened it to reveal a large room with many empty tables and chairs and an old lady behind the bar. "Welcome weary travelers," the old lady said, "rest your bones and I will bring you a cold refreshing drink." And she went into the back room.

"Something is strange," said Jemma, "the horses are out, but no one is here. Be on guard." The old lady returned with four goblets of cold beer. Jake and Lya drank deeply while Sam and Jemma requested water. The old lady looked surprised and insisted they drink the beer, but both insisted they wanted water. So, she poured them glasses from the goblet on the bar and they both drank deeply. A few minutes later, Jake and Lya passed out. Sam and Jemma knew immediately that the beer had been drugged. Sam grabbed the old bar-lady by her collar, "What was in the beer, you old hag?" he asked.

"Nothing, my boy, it's just strong beer and your weak friends could not handle it," she smiled showing three rotten teeth and one white one.

"Don't lie to me, woman, I have no qualms killing you here and now," Sam threatened. Just then, the main door opened, and two burly men walked in. They seemed angry and ready for a fight. They went for Sam, but Jemma leapt and met them halfway with a ruby-bright red sword in her hand.

"One step further and you lose your legs," she said calmly. The two men both took a step forward. Jemma seemed to twitch, and nothing happened. Then a trickle of blood ran down both men from right under their knees. Both men screamed in agony as they fell on the floor, but their forward legs stayed where they were. A clamor was heard in the upper floor and some from below. It sounded like a battalion was coming at them. Sam threw the old hag across the room, carried Jake and Lya under his arms and ran to the horses with Jemma leading the way. They flopped Lya on one horse and Jake on the other, mounted their steeds and sped off into the night.

As they galloped, Jemma heard Jake and Lya moan. She looked back to check if either had fallen off and saw they were waking up. She looked further behind and saw no one in pursuit, so, she slowed her horse with Sam, keeping pace until they got to a full stop. She dismounted and checked on Lya while Sam helped Jake to his feet.

"What a headache!" Jake said, "That beer must have one hell of a kick!" Jake looked around. "Where are we?"

"The old hag drugged you," said Jemma. "We got you out of there and are on our way to the resting place you told us about." As she finished, they heard the sound of wolves howling nearby. Sam got ready and a shimmer started appearing in his hand when Jemma shouted, "Stop! We might be able to kill them, but the horses will run regardless. Unless you want to finish this journey on foot, I suggest we try to get to the resting place before we have to walk there."

"Good point," said Sam and without adding any other words, jumped on his horse and waited for the others to mount theirs. A minute later he bellowed loud "hiyaa" and all four horses took off towards the resting place. As the sun was about to rise and shafaq hue covered the land, they saw the resting place ahead. Tired and weary, the four travelers made their way there to find a large stable and a young man receiving their horses and guiding them in. The resting place was a brick-building of three stories and a basement. The roof had interesting openings which Jake explained let the hot air out; thus, always driving in cooler air and keeping the building cool. "It's like reverse chimneys," he had explained. As they walked in, Sam saw a large sign over the doubled oak-door reading: *'Resting Place'*.

--

Clemence, a red headed man who had only arrived half an hour ago had just gotten his drink when he turned to Greg, a bald bearded man and sighed, "Ugh, these trips are starting to kill me, Greg. Travelling between the Free Tribes and Vegna every month is really taking a toll on me and my horse. If only Brenda and kids would move there, things would be much easier."

"I hear you brother," answered Greg. "Now that the war is over, maybe they would consider moving, and better yet, we can take the shortcut through Sanctuary which would shave a day and a half off travelling." Just then the double oak-door of the resting place opened and in walked a large muscular man with purple eyes, followed by a tall blond beauty, also with purple eyes. A few steps behind walked a beautiful brunette holding the hand of a wide shouldered man. They walked to the bar and the large muscular man sat on the stool by Clemence and ordered an ale while the remaining three found an empty table and sat down. As the bartender brought the ale, the large man asked him if they have any rooms for rent. The bartender pointed him towards the manager who was sitting at the end of the bar, counting on his fingers.

Sam walked to the manager who greeted him with a smile. "Do you have rooms for the day?" Sam asked. "We need four."

"I am sorry, good sir, but we only have three left," answered the manager.

"Fine, we will take them," said Sam realizing that he might be the one sharing. When he joined Jemma, Lya and Jake at the table, he told them about the rooms and immediately Jemma and Lya said, "We will bunk together," at the same time. Feeling relieved, Sam ushered for the waitress to get them something to eat.

"This is the first time I have dinner for breakfast," joked Jake as the first sun had just risen and they were planning to sleep.

"That's interesting," chimed Lya while Sam smiled and drank his ale and Jemma started eating. A few minutes later, the dining hall started emptying out with people going up or down to their rooms to sleep for the day and get energy to travel through the night. Being the last ones to arrive, Sam, Jemma, Lya and Jake were the last ones to leave their table to head to their rooms. Jemma and Lya were talking up a storm on their way to their room upstairs while Jake and Sam walked in silence to their rooms in the basement. As Jake got to his door, he smiled at Sam and said, "Good day," in an effort to twist day and night. Sam turned to him and smiled then turned to walk away. After a second, Sam stopped and turned back to Jake.

"Lya seems nice. Be good to her," he said and turned and headed for his room.

Sam was sitting in the big hall with the Bear crest on top of it. His mother had just told him to call his sister. He walked through the door to see a small fountain in front of the hall. By the fountain was a little girl looking into the pond and babbling to the fish. The only word that made sense from her babbles was "fwend." He wanted to call her but did not know her name. He stood there in silence thinking of what to do.

The girl then looks at him and puts her arms out, with her fingers opening and closing and squeals, "Ham! Ham!" Sam walks over to her, looking at her large purple eyes and huge smile and tries to pick her up to carry her inside but loses his footing and falls into the fountain.

Sam woke up covered in sweat. *"What a strange dream,"* he thought. *"Must be the heat getting to me!"* As he was underground, he had no clue what the time was. So, he washed his face, got dressed and walked out of his room hoping it was almost sundown. There was little to no sound around and he guessed it was still daytime. He climbed the stairs to the dining hall to see that a few other people were sitting there eating. "What time is it?" he asked a red headed man at a table, who was eating eggs and bacon. The bald bearded man next to him answered, "Almost sundown. Why don't you join us?"

Sam was about to answer when Jemma and Lya walked into the hall and called him to join them. "Thank you for your offer, but my friends are here," he said and walked over to the girls and joined them at their table. A waiter passed by and took their order, and Lya ordered an extra meal for Jake.

A few minutes later, Jake arrived along with the food. The four ate in silence and then Sam broke that silence with, "Are we ready to go? It's already dark outside." The four nodded in agreement and they all got up and walked over to the door to ask for their horses. When the horses arrived and the bill had been paid, by Jake, who insisted, the travelers resumed their journey to Vegna. It was still a full moon, so they had little trouble seeing the way. By the time it was sunrise, they had reached the gates of Vegna. The massive gates were made of redwood and had three giant bars placed horizontally on them as reinforcement. The gates were at least 20 meters high and on top was a walkway where sentries stood and looked over the desert. *This is one kingdom only a fool would attack,* thought Sam, *it's impenetrable.* As he was marveling at the brick walls and architecture, a guard called out, "Jake, is that you?"

Jake got flustered and tried to keep his composure, "Bran, hey buddy, long time no see. How have you been?" Bran walked towards Jake and when he got closer, he swung at him. Jake ducked and avoided the punch but did not hit back. Sam stepped in and held Bran by the shoulders, pinning him in place.

"What is your beef with my friend?" Sam asked.

Before Bran could answer, Jake put his hand on Sam's shoulder and said, "Bran is Melinda's husband and I had made life a little difficult for them. I was jealous that she chose him." Jake said with his eyes lowered, but then he raised his head and with a smile said, "But that is all ancient history now." He looked at Lya, smiled further and said, "Turns out, Bran did me a service!"

Bran, still unable to move, said, "Well, seems we should let bygones be bygones. Maybe we can have beer later, Jake. That is if you don't plant me in this spot, sir," he said, looking at Sam.

Sam smiled and let him go saying, "You have a good sense of humor. Maybe a beer with you isn't a bad idea after all. But before we get all friendly, we passed a place on the way here that is obviously a travelers' trap. We made it out by luck," he said turning to Jemma, then back to Bran, "you need to send some soldiers there to get these bandits."

Bran smiled and said, "We heard of that last night and are sending a troop there today. It seems many people here are waiting on some people who have disappeared."

"Good luck then," said Sam and walked back to his horse. Soon the travelers entered Vegna from the main gate to see this desert city.

Chapter 7
Vegna

Having lost his memory, Sam did not know what to expect in Vegna. Judging from the desert trip he had taken, he expected a very hot environment, sand everywhere and lots of dust. What he saw was completely different. Upon entering Vegna, and at the gate, he was greeted with a jet of cool air coming from above. It ruffled his long hair a bit, but it was a welcoming and refreshing surprise. Once past the gate, Sam saw a large fountain in the middle of an oval shaped grass patch. People were sitting on the grass, enjoying the cool breeze and the sun. Sam looked around to find the source of the cool breeze and noticed that the area had statues of animals with their mouths open and jets of cool air coming from them, making the whole area cool and breezy. Beyond the green area was a large brick building and the word "library" written above the doors. The building had many windows on the upper three floors. To the left and right of the building were streets that looked like they were made of brick and cement, making them very flat and comfortable to walk on. The sides of the streets were adorned with flowers and bushes cut to geometrical shapes.

Jake led the way down the street to the right of the library and Sam looked all around to find something to jog his memory. It seemed that the streets and houses were designed in squares making each section a block. Sam counted four blocks before they came to an open grassed area.

"This is a Vegna Park," said Jake proudly. "I used to play here as a kid," he added.

Lya was taking everything in and every time she saw something interesting, she would whisper it to Jake. Jemma had been here recently, so she was not overwhelmed by the city. Jake walked to the right to a vendor who was selling food.

"Four with everything," he asked the salesman who handed him four tubular-looking bread rolls with what seemed to Sam was a cylinder of meat with red and yellow sauces on it.

"This is a Vegna delicacy, you can only find it here. They call it 'street food'," said Jake. "Give it a taste and see what you think."

Sam bit into the food carefully, then his eyes widened and said, "Daaaamn…this is amazing," with a full mouth that Jake almost didn't understand it. Jemma and Lya bit into their food and enjoyed each bite. Sam then asked Jake, "What do they call this?"

"Hot Dog," said Jake.

Sam's face turned and was about to spit out the food when Jake quickly added, "It's not made of dogs! It's made of chicken or pork or beef, but they called it hot dog because that is what the recipe, they found called it. Apparently, it was found in an archeological dig near here."

"I heard about this," said Jemma, "when I was last here, they had mentioned that they found very interesting things in this dig. I think they mentioned something called *crossant* or *coissent*. Not sure. But the story goes that they could not decipher the script, so they have not tried to make it. But the hot dog—that recipe worked."

Sam, being relieved that he was not eating dogs, finished his food and asked for another which was quickly delivered and devoured.

"Now that we are fed, let me take you to where we will be resting and sleeping," said Jake who led the way to the left of the green park. A few minutes later, they were in front of a massive building. It was four stories high and long enough to fit five houses. "This is a hotel," said Jake. "It's like an inn, but with larger rooms and something called room service. This means they fix up…"

"We know what a hotel is," interrupted Sam. "Seriously, Jake, you are trying too hard!"

Jake smiled and ushered them in. Jemma and Lya decided that they want to be on the top floor to get the best views of the city while Jake and Sam took lower floors as they wanted to be close to their rooms when they come back drunk or tired! Then, all four of them went to their rooms to bathe and change. Sam's room was large with a large bed in the center. The bed had two nightstands, one on each side, and in the corner of the room was a soft and comfortable sofa. There was a curtain covering another part of the room where Sam stayed. He opened the curtain to find a smaller room which was meant to be a water closet…as he examined it, he saw a bath which he noticed was already filled with hot water and smelt of lavender. Sam considered the thought of a bath for a few seconds and then undressed and sat in the bath, feeling all the stress of the journey dissolve in the water.

Sam was sitting in the garden with his parents. Suddenly, four horsemen show up on black horses. The horses had red eyes that shone, and their breath was smokey. Two men jumped from their horses only to be met by Sam's mother's sickle while the other two had been decapitated by his father's sword. A black arrow with yellow feathers whooshed by Sam's face to land in his mother's chest. His father ran to her only to be stopped by a similar arrow to his chest. Sam was paralyzed. He heard a baby cry and the man that was coming for him turned away. Sam found the courage and jumped up and ran. Sam ran towards the cliff. He heard footsteps behind him chasing him and he jumped. He fell through trees and his right thigh was slashed by one of the broken branches. He landed with a thud by a large tree that had a little hole in it, like a burrow for a large fox. He crawled in and bit on a piece of wood so as not to scream from the pain in his leg. He was waiting there for the attackers to leave. When it got dark, a porcupine showed up at the doorway of the burrow trying to get in, and Sam had to beat it with the stick he was biting on. The porcupine turned to run, but only after sending some of its quills into the little boy. Sam turned to pick the quills.

Sam jumped out of the bath, looking for the quills in his body.

"Oh my," he exclaimed out loud, "what a dream! Or was this another memory." Nevertheless, he was sure it was a memory and decided to share it with Jemma, Lya and Jake with the hopes they would like to know what was happening.

He dried himself with the towel provided with the room and put on the clothes that he got from Paul in the Kiaff inn. Sam walked out of his room to see Jake walking towards him with a look of concern on his face.

"What's the matter," he asked Jake.

"You had been in there for too long and we were getting worried," Jake answered.

"Oh, sorry about that, I fell asleep in the bath!" said Sam. "This lavender really relaxes you!" Jake and Sam walked downstairs to the main lobby where Jemma and Lya were waiting.

"About time you showed up," said Jemma.

"Yeah, you had us worried," said Lya.

"Sorry about that," said Sam. "I fell asleep in the bath and had the weirdest dream."

"Okay, tell us about it as we walk," said Jake. "We need to meet someone who might have some information for Jemma," he added.

As they left the hotel, Sam told them about his dream, his parents, the raiders and the scar on his leg. None of them knew where the cliff from his dream might be.

"It could be in Kiaff, Vegna or with the free tribes," said Jemma. "This does not help at all!"

Then Jake, who was leading the way stopped in front of an old house that looked like it was recently restored. It was made of brick, had a large green door and a spacious garden in front of it. He opened the garden gate and proceeded to walk in when a dog showed up from nowhere and started barking at him. Jake jumped back and closed the gate quickly.

"That's one way to announce our arrival," he joked with a shaky voice.

A few seconds later, a lady opened the door and shouted, "Enough, Nitro!" and the dog went silent and walked away.

"We are here to talk to Scarlett," shouted Jake from the gate. "She is expecting us."

"I sure am," replied the lady with a strange accent. "Y'all wanna come in?"

As they walked into the garden, Scarlett suddenly turned to Sam and said, "Sam, is that you? Hot damn I missed you boy, come here, and give me some sugar." And she threw her arms around the surprised giant man who instinctively hugged her back. Scarlett was a medium height woman who still retained her beauty even though she seemed old to her visitors, she was in her early fifties but had looked after herself well. She was a voluptuous woman and dressed to flaunt her features but still kept an air of class around her. She had been widowed long ago and lived on her own. Her husband had left her a few properties which she managed well, allowing her to buy others and grow her real estate business. Once her monthly rent income was enough to give her the life she wanted, she retired and spent her days doing whatever she felt like that day. To many of her neighbors, she was eccentric, but to those that knew her, she was just a woman who loved life and wanted to live it all before she moved on.

"I am sorry, Ma'am," said Sam, "but I lost my memory and do not know who you are."

"Well, my boy, this is truly sad to hear," said Scarlett. "But the interesting thing is, that I know you. You came here a few years ago and built a relationship with the King. Even though the kingdom was at war. The King believed you when you told him that you have no opinion of the war besides that it is a lose-lose situation. Recently, you left Vegna with the aim to stop the last battle because you had information both sides should hear. You never told anyone this information, but it was enough for the King to let you go to try to stop the battle. When you didn't return, he thought you died, but I knew you were going to be fine. My friendly purple-eyed giant who saved me from those thugs."

"What thugs," asked Jake, secretly hoping it wasn't him or his friends.

"Oh, street thugs here in Vegna. But not to worry, they are in jail now since Sam here knocked all three of them out cold and called for the guards to come and get them."

Sam, hoping that she knows more asked, "Do you know more about my history?"

"I wish I did," Scarlett answered, "but I only know you from when you were here. You never spoke of your past."

"Well, it's something to start with," said Sam.

Then Jake remembered they were there to ask for Jemma, "We wanted to ask you about a man with a scar on his face, two colored eyes and a redheaded woman with green eyes." This was all he could remember from the story Jemma had told them of what Paul, the innkeeper, in Kiaff said.

"Oh, I met them once, many years ago. Vile creatures. They had a little girl with them who they didn't let play with anyone. Cute little thing too. They pretended to be her father and nanny, but it was clear neither of them loved that girl. She must have been three or four when I met them. They stayed in the Vegna Royal hotel for a few days and wanted to rent one of my properties. That man did not know how to take no for an answer!" She laughed. "The woman always carried a

70

bow with her. As if she was going into battle any minute. And to think she claimed to be a nanny. Pushah!"

"Anything else you can tell us?" asked Jemma. "I'm sorry honey, that's all I remember" answered Scarlett. The four got up to leave and Scarlett said, "Why don't y'all stay for dinner? I am making a pot roast tonight."

"Thank you for the invitation, Ma'am," said Sam, "but I want to talk to the King." And with that they got up and left.

When they were back on the street, Jemma turned to Sam and said, "King, eh? Who knew you were from high places and not even a tail-lace in sight?"

"I knew he had to be royalty," said Lya. "There was something royal about him," she said turning to Jake who just shrugged. They walked for a few blocks until they got a massive gate.

"This must be the palace," said Sam.

"Nope, it's the second level of Vegna," said Jemma.

"How many levels before we got to the king?" asked Sam.

"One more," answered Jake.

As they walked to the second level, they noticed that the houses were bigger than in the first level and the gardens wider with statues in them. It felt that the further in they moved from the gates, the richer the people were. Finally, they got to a castle with guards at the gate and sentries on the wall.

"That must be it," said Sam turning to Jake who nodded. Then a booming voice called out, "SAM! You made it!"

Chapter 8
The King

King Roy walked over to Sam with his arms stretched wide and embraced him with a bear hug. The King let go of Sam and grabbed Sam's right hand in a firm handshake, and his left hand went to Jemma's shoulder and softly squeezed it three times with no one noticing. Jemma knew what it meant, but the others had not seen the quick and stealthy move. The King was a well-built man, almost as well built as Sam. He wore a brown tunic, leather leggings and polished boots. A few seconds later, four breathless guards showed up and stood by the King. "Gave them the slip," said the young King laughing and patting Sam on the shoulder. Then he turned to Jake, Jemma and Lya who had been standing there silently and said, "If you are friends of Sam's, you are welcome here. Come, let's go inside. Sam, we have a lot to catch up on." Leading the way, the King walked through the castle gate and onto the castle grounds.

People around were bowing as they walked by and many started whispering when they saw Sam, Jemma, Jake and Lya walking behind him. They got to an area in the garden that was away from the king's court. There was a large canopy under which were wooden carved chairs with cushions and a table full of fruits and desserts. The King sat on the largest of the chairs and signaled to the rest to sit down as well. Jake, being hungry, walked to the table with the fruits. Lya, feeling embarrassed by his actions whispered loudly, "Jake."

The King heard her and to alleviate her embarrassment said to Jake and the rest, "Please eat, it will go rotten if no one eats it." Then he turned to Sam, "I know the battle happened, but the war ended. Did you tell them what you knew?"

Sam lowered his head and said, "I don't know. All I remember is waking up on the battlefield and seeing dead knights around me. I have no memory from before then." The King looked shocked, but then laughed and said, "Well, in that case, you never beat me at arm wrestling," and laughed even louder.

"But, your majesty," said Sam, "What was the thing I wanted to tell them."

The King laughed even harder and said, "You want to tell me that you do not remember finding out that the disputed lands were neither ours nor theirs? That the free tribes actually owned their lands? Isn't that why you are here with Jemma?"

Sam was surprised that the King knew Jemma. Jemma on the other hand looked up at the King and said, "When were you planning on telling me that you know!"

"I found out right after you left here," said the King. "Sam had just come back with the news. Did you know?" he asked with an accusing tone.

"I did," she said, "but telling either you or Kiaff that the free tribes owned the land, would have made us part of a war we wanted nothing to do with," replied Jemma, "and the land in question is barren, so I weighed its value over that of our warrior's lives. I didn't even tell my father." Knowing that showing emotion in public would no longer affect the war,

73

Roy got up from his chair and walked to Jemma, held her by the shoulders and kissed her. She wrapped her arms around him and kissed him back. Sam and Jake looked at them with shock while Lya smiled and held her hands to her heart. Then Lya's face got suddenly serious as if she figured something out, she looked at Jemma, "If you have been visiting here and Sam stayed here, shouldn't you two know each other?"

"They were never here at the same time. And most of the time when Jemma was here, she stayed in the diplomatic quarters where Sam never went," replied the King staring into Jemma's eyes.

Feeling that they are now invading a romantic moment between the King and Jemma, Jake got up and said, "We will take your leave now, your majesty."

"Nonsense," said the King turning towards them and keeping his arm around Jemma's waist, "You will stay here as my guests. Sam and Jemma both have rooms here, and we can surely find you each a room. Unless you prefer one?" he said winking at Jake who blushed.

"Two rooms are better, your majesty," said Jake.

"Then it's settled," said the King walking away with Jemma, holding her hand.

"See you at dinner," And with that they were gone. Sam turned to Jake and Lya saying, "She did mention she had a diplomatic connection here, but the King!"

Sam sat in his luxury room in the castle. The room was large with a four-post-bed in the middle of it facing the door. Behind the bed was a window on each side and under each window was a bedside table. On each bedside table was a candle standing in an ornate holder. On the right wall of the room was a large fireplace which was cleaned and had logs in it set in a way to quickly start a fire and burn slowly. Sam wondered why a fireplace is needed in the desert. On the opposite side of the room was a wardrobe and a chest of drawers which were made from dark wood and polished to a shine. Next to them were three polished boots set neatly there, but one of them seemed to be worn more than the others. It crossed Sam's mind that maybe these must have been his favorite boots. On the far side of the room, Sam noticed a small curtain covering the corner. He walked to the curtain, slid it open to reveal another room that had a bath, a washing basin and toilet. On the wall was a mirror and a shelf underneath it that had a razor on it. Sam walked to the mirror and looked at his beard, "I think I will keep it," he said out loud as he ran his hands over it.

Moving back into the main chamber, Sam walked to the wardrobe and opened it with the hopes of finding something that could jog his memory about his origins. He sifted through his clothes and found nothing interesting beside a small bag of Lavender which the staff must have kept there to keep scorpions out and to give a nice aroma to his clothes. He then turned his attention to the chest of drawers. In the top drawer, he found leggings in different fabrics and colors. In the second drawer, he found a hairbrush, a comb, and some hair ties. Sam was giving up when he opened the third and last drawer in the chest of drawers. But a shiny tail-lace caught his eye in the corner of the drawer tucked behind what seemed to be towels. He took out the tail-lace and examined it. It looked old, yet still had its golden shine. The size of the item was too small for a grownup, but it would fit a child perfectly. Children do not usually get tail-laces unless they are children of tribe

75

leaders or royalty. He wondered how he got to have this rare item. The engraving on the tail-lace was almost rubbed out, but it looked like a bear. Remembering his recurring dream, Sam was sure this was his and that his parents must have been tribe leaders, as his dream of their death does not peg them as royalty. He remembered that Jake had promised to take him to the hall in his dreams and set out to find him in the vast castle.

Sam left his room on the third floor of the castle but did not know which way to go! There was one more floor above him and two below, and Jake could be on any of them. He decided to start on the top floor and work his way down. Upon reaching the top floor from the staircase, Sam could hear sounds of people talking. The voices were that of one man and one woman. Sam thought that it could be Lya and Jake, but something in his gut told him not to call out to them but to walk silently to the location of the sound. The hallway was long and there were doors on opposite sides of the hall. About five doors on each side and a last door at the end of the hallway. The floor was carpeted, making creeping around an easier task. Sam made it to the first door on the right only to realize that the voices of the two people in there were not Jake and Lya, but two strange voices.

He was walking away from the door when a sentence by the woman got his attention, "How do you plan to poison the King when we can't even get close to his food? I am telling you, an arrow through the heart will get the job done and we can be far away giving us a head start."

"But an arrow confirms he was killed," said the man. "We need to make it look like he got sick and died. That way, there will be no suspicion and we can walk around freely, and no one is the wiser."

Hearing this, Sam decided to find out who these people are and to alert the King of the plot. He went down one flight of steps and waited at the landing between the stairs for them to leave the room.

A few minutes later, very well-dressed man and lady walked out of the room, Sam made it look like he was climbing the stairs. As they passed him, he took a good look at their faces and said with a puff, "Four stories up. It's a killer." The well-dressed man smiled but the lady ignored him, though Sam was overwhelmed by the strong perfume she was wearing. He continued to the top of the stairs and walked around the hallway to complete the ruse and to see if he could find Jake. But Jake's room was not there. Sam then went to the second floor and walked down the hallway hoping that Jake would have left his door open, but again he had no luck. As Sam got to the first floor, he saw Jake in the hallway, standing in front of a closed door.

"Hey Jake," said Sam, "I was looking for you. Is this your room?"

"No," said Jake. "This is Lya's room, and I am waiting for her to get ready, so we can go out and I can show her the places I had promised her."

"Okay, well, I need your help with something. Got a minute to spare?" said Sam.

"Sure," said Jake and then knocked on Lya's door and spoke through it, "Sweety, I will be downstairs with Sam when you are done."

"Okay, honey," came the answer from behind the door.

Sam walked with Jake to an empty corner and told him what he had heard in the room. Jake kept a cool composure and asked Sam to identify these people. Sam looked around but could not find them. The two of them then walked slowly through the ground floor of the castle lobby, through the large white doors and down the steps into the garden. In the distance, they saw the canopy they sat under. On the right and left, there were people from the King's court walking about or sitting on benches or standing together in groups talking. Sam checked each face and none of them looked like the ones he had seen. Thinking that they might have left the grounds, they walked in to find Lya waiting by the door. She was wearing a red dress that was tight at the waist but had ruffles at the bottom. On her feet, Lya wore a pair of black high heeled platform shoes. To Jake, she was the embodiment of beauty. When they got closer to her, Jake could smell the fruity perfume she had on, which immediately earned its position as the best perfume he had ever smelt.

"Shall we?" said Lya with a smile.

"Yes, Milady. We shall," said Jake holding out his elbow for Lya to per her arm through and they walked away arm in arm with Jake winking at Sam.

As Sam turned to walk into the castle, he saw a door in the corner of the lobby open and the woman he had seen on the top floor walking fast towards the stairs. She was walking alone and looked flustered and was walking in a hurry. Sam thought of following her but was too curious to see where she had come from. He walked to the door she came out of and peaked in. It was the palace kitchen. He was sure that the poison plan was on, and that they will be poisoning the King today. Sam walked in as if he was lost and saw the man from the top floor walking near some Danish pastry.

The cook then walked in, looked at the man and said, "Lord Jimmy, please leave these Danishes alone. They are for the King. You do know he likes his Danishes." She ended with a polite yet fake smile.

Jimmy turned to her, smiled and said, "Of course, my dear. I just wanted to taste one. But I think I will get a chance after dinner tonight." He smiled and walked out of the same door the cook walked in. Sam had not been noticed, but he knew their plan for the evening.

Being early for dinner and remembering the tail-lace he had found in his room, Sam thought of going to the royal library in the palace to see if he could find a book about family sigils. He walked over to a serving maid and asked her where the royal library was. As she was giving him directions, he noticed that she smelt exactly as strong as the lady from the top floor that ignored him on the stairs. He took a good look at her only to realize it was the same woman. Not showing that he recognized her, Sam thanked her and went towards the library. As he entered the library doors, Sam was astonished by the number of shelves and books that the library held. Sam wondered if each of these books was read, or better yet, if anyone had read at least half of these books in one lifetime. Sam walked around the library looking for the section on families and sigils when he bumped into Jemma.

"Hey," he said. "What are you doing here?"

"What do you mean? I love books and reading," said Jemma. "This is where I can learn new things, travel to new and distant worlds or find out more about this one."

"Wow," said Sam, "that was very poetic."

She smiled and then asked, "What brings you here? I didn't take you for the reading type. No offense."

Sam was not bothered, it was true, he did not like reading much. But then he told her about the tail-lace he found and wanted to know more about the bear clan. Jemma walked with him past a few shelves and then handed him a massive book.

"Here you go," she said. "This should have the answers you seek."

As she turned to leave, Sam grabbed her by the hand, pulled her close and whispered what he knew about the assassination attempt on the King. Jemma looked very angry, "If Roy dies, my life will end with him. Tell me who the assassins are, and I shall dispose of them."

"Don't even get close," said Sam. "You are still of the free tribes, and this can create an incident. Tell the King, and I will also be there, and I have a plan." Jemma turned and left in a hurry while Sam moved to the closest reading table, sat down and opened the book, setting it on the table.

A couple of hours later, a serving girl walked up to Sam, who was reading the book Jemma had given him and paying extra attention to one page, and said, "Excuse me sir, but dinner will be served soon, and you are expected."

Sam jumped from his seat as she gave him a fright. He turned to her, thanked her, got up and walked away with the book tucked under his arm. When Sam got to the dining hall, Jemma was already there sitting on the first chair to the right of the King who had not yet arrived. Jake and Lya were there as well as some of the king's court whom Sam did not know. But he did see Jimmy sitting at the table between two elderly ladies. A serving girl ushered Sam to his seat which was opposite Jemma's. He could see that Jemma was less worried, but he smiled at her confirming that he had a plan. A few minutes later, the King walked in. Everyone stood where they sat, as he walked to his chair. "Sit down," he said to everyone with a smile. As he sat, he held Jemma's hand, drew it to his lips and kissed it softly.

Jemma blushed. The King then patted Sam on the shoulder and whispered, "How was your search?" Sam was surprised that the King knew where he was and looked at Jemma who smiled guiltily. Then it was time to serve the food. The serving team delivered a plate in front of each of the guests. As they placed the plates in front of the King and his guests, Sam noticed the serving girl who placed the plate in front of the King was none other than the lady he met on the stairs. He was about to tell the King about the plot when the King suddenly announced, "Today is going to be a special dinner. Today, I proposed to the greatest woman in the world, and she said yes!" He smiled. Some people at the table gasped, others smiled, but all clapped. The King continued, "For that, I have decided that we should all celebrate and as such, today, the serving team will join us for dinner."

Everyone at the table looked horrified at this idea, but no one dared speak out. The serving team then brought chairs and sat in between the guests silently, each bringing their own plate of soup with them. The king then got up carrying his plate of soup and said, "And since this is your day, I want to give you my bowl of soup," and placed it in front of the serving girl who delivered the same plate to him. "Eat up my dears, for today is a special day." Sam saw the serving girl panic and look towards Jimmy who seemed unfazed. "Eat up, my dear," said the King to the serving girl. With a shaking hand, she took the spoon and collected the soup from the dish and very slowly lifted it to her mouth all the while looking at Jimmy who was still not bothered. Then she dropped the spoon in her plate and shouted at Jimmy, "I could die!"

Jimmy looked at her with shock, "What are you saying to me, servant girl? How dare you address me this way!"

The look of heartbreak on her face told the whole story. Seeing this, the King then took the bowl and placed it in front of Jimmy.

"Have some of mine, Jimmy," the King said.

Jimmy's mouth started shaking and he looked at the King stuttering "I-I-I-I" when he was interrupted by the dining hall door opening loudly and six guards walking in.

"You know what to do," said the King pointing at stuttering Jimmy and the crying lady. Neither Jimmy nor the lady said anything when the guards grabbed them, but as they were being dragged out of the dining hall, the lady started screaming, "Your majesty, spare me and I will tell you everything." But the guards kept dragging her and the King didn't listen. The King then turned to all the guests and said, "Now that the assassination attempt is over, let's go out to the garden where the cooks have prepared a spit and are roasting meat on it as we speak. And..." He paused. "...it's not poisoned." All the guests got up and walked in a single file out of the dining hall.

Chapter 9
Of bears and bells

Sam was sitting in the library reading a family insignia book when Jemma and Lya joined him.

"Any luck?" asked Lya.

"I think so," said Sam pointing at the page he was on. Lya could see that there was a drawing of the same tail-lace he had in his hand which was similar to Jake's in design. "According to this book, this is the sign of one of the free tribes. But the whole tribe was killed off a long time ago," said Sam. "They were a tribe of warriors that had been there for ages," he continued, "but somehow, they got eradicated suddenly and no one knows how or why. The book speaks of a few survivors, but they were too few and no one has seen them or heard of them. It's like they disappeared."

"Ooh, I have heard of such a tribe," said Lya. "When I was little, I was always getting into fights. One day, my father told me about this tribe as a lesson that if you fight too many people, one day they will all gang up on you and you will surely lose this fight."

"Did you know the tribe's name?" asked Sam. "The book does not really give them one."

Lya thought for a moment and then said, "I don't think they even had a name, just warriors, I guess."

Feeling a bit disappointed, Sam closed the book and got up saying, "It seems this is all I can get from here. I might need to go to the free tribes for more information." With that, the three walked out of the royal library, through the palace and into the palace gardens where Jake and King Roy were having tea under the canopy.

"Any luck buddy," asked Jake.

"Nothing much, but all roads lead to the free tribes," said Sam.

"Well, then join us for a tea and let's make a plan," said the King. This was a welcome break for Sam who had spent most of the last three days in the library with the books.

During afternoon tea, most of the discussion was planning for Roy and Jemma's wedding. Then Lya asked, "How did you propose, your majesty?"

The King smiled at Lya and said, "As the maid of honor, you can call me Roy when we are not in company of strangers or dignitaries."

Lya's face lit up while Jemma's blushed. "Maid of Honor? Really?" squealed Lya.

"I was about to ask you," said Jemma blushing, "...but hadn't had the time. And you," she said softly punching Roy's shoulder, "should have checked with me."

"Sorry, honey," said Roy sheepishly with a smile.

"But I still want to know how you proposed," said a really excited Lya.

"Well, the day you came, we went for a long walk by the lake," said Roy. "I slipped and was about to fall into the lake when Jemma pushed me in. Then she jumped in after me

84

laughing. I loved Jemma, but at that moment I was sure this is my queen. We swam for a bit and got out. We lit a fire and hung our clothes to dry. It was the perfect setting for a man to propose to a woman, not a King to a chief's daughter. I got on one knee and asked her if she would be the wife of a man and she said yes." Roy took a deep breath and continued, "When we got dressed, I was King again, I knelt down and as a King proposed to a chief's daughter, and she said yes again."

Jemma got up and grabbed Lya's hand, then she knelt down and asked, "Will you be my maid of honor, as a friend and songstress at the wedding?"

Lya had tears in her eyes when she said, "A thousand times yes." Jemma got up and they hugged tightly.

Sam was waiting for an hour when Jake finally arrived. "Sorry Sam, Lya needed me for something," Jake said out of breath as he had been running.

"You promised to take me to the hall with the bear crest," Sam reminded him. "Now is the best time. Lead the way."

Jake took a deep breath and said, "and I intend to keep my word. Let's go get the horses as it is a fair distance from here." And the two walked towards the stable. Once there, they got on their horses and rode west. A few minutes passed by and the houses around them became smaller signaling that they were leaving the rich quarters. As they rode, Sam noticed that the Kingdom of Vegna was much bigger than he thought, for he could not see the perimeter wall in the distance even though he could see the horizon. Then, on the horizon, Sam saw a small round structure with a thatch roof. The closer they got, the more details he could see. From the outside, the structure looked like one large round room. It was surprisingly white, as if painted only yesterday. There was a dry fountain in front of it but the statue in the middle was broken. The place looked deserted. The two men got off their horses and walked inside the round hall. Even though the temperature was hot outside, it was surprisingly cool inside. The floors were made of granite and shone like a mirror; however, they were covered with dust. The round hall had six pillars in it, holding up the ceiling that was also granite.

"Why is there thatch if the ceiling is granite?" asked Sam.

"Oh, I think for insulation against the heat," answered Jake, "but I do not know for sure."

As Sam turned to face the door, he saw the Bear crest atop of it, just like in his dreams. He followed the path of his dream to the fountain, seeing the dream in one eye and reality in the other. He then turned to the right and walked a few paces and stomped on the ground. The ground made a hollow sound.

"There was something important hidden down here," he said to Jake. "I don't know what, but I know it is there." Jake pulled out his hunting knife and dug it into the ground. The knife hit a plank of wood. A few minutes later, they had cleared the sand and removed a couple of wooden planks and were peering inside. Jake put his hand through and pulled out what was in the secret hole; it was a leather scroll. He unrolled it to reveal a map of their known world. A red line ran from what seemed to be their location, through Vegna, via Sanctuary, through Kiaff and ending in an area within the free tribes with a small drawing of a bear by the free tribes. The bear looked very similar to the design of the bear on Sam's tail-lace. Jake pulled out his and it was also the same.

Back at the castle, Jemma and Lya were in deep discussion when Jake and Sam returned. The two men told them about the hall and showed them the map. Jemma said

86

she knew where the area was and described how to get there. "There is a river that runs fast in all seasons," she said, "…and there is no bridge to cross it. This location is right behind that river. If you plan to go there, you will need to be very careful. Almost no one ever tried crossing it," she ended.

"Well, I am sure I am going there," said Sam.

"I will come too," said Jake. "It might be relevant to me too," he said with his hand holding his tail-lace in his pocket.

"Well, if you leave soon," said Lya. "I will go with you to Sanctuary to settle my business there. Jemma has asked me to move here as the royal bard and promised a job for Jake too if he wants one. Sorry Jake, I haven't had a chance to tell you earlier." She ended with a smile and a blush.

"I was going to ask if you would consider moving here as well," said Jake excitedly. "I have an offer, but I will happily take whatever job you have for me," he said to Jemma.

"We will find something for your skills," smiled Jemma who then turned to Sam and said, "You need no invite Sam, this is and will always be a home for you." Sam smiled and bowed slightly as an acknowledgement and a thank you.

Sam left them and walked back to his room with the map to study it further. He could see that the map was very meticulously made as it showed every part of the land. He even saw shortcuts he knew and many he did not. The map also showed images of certain creatures which prevailed in certain areas; he saw a drawing of a scorpion in the desert, a furry creature in the woods, a strange snake in a river and a confusing creature in the mountains which lead to the free tribes. He did not ever remember going there, so he was curious as to what this animal was. "I guess I will find out soon enough," he said out loud as he rolled the map up. Sam walked over to the window that overlooked the garden and looked out at the world as the second sun was about to set. He then turned his gaze to the palace garden and saw Jake standing with Lya there. It looked like they were having an argument. Lya turned away to leave when Jake reached out and grabbed her by the arm. She swung at him, but he saw it coming and ducked. Then Jake took a step back and knelt on one knee producing something from his pocket. Lya put both hands to her mouth, then put out her hand. It looked like he was proposing. *That's a strange way to start a proposal,* Sam thought to himself as he saw Jake stand back up and Lya jump into his arms. He watched as they held each other for a while, then he turned and walked to the bed and sat down. Sam was happy for Lya and Jake as he always thought they looked good together, but he did feel a tinge of jealousy not having found someone himself. He was sure he did not have anyone, because if he did have someone, they would have found him by now. He then got up and started packing his duffle for their upcoming trip.

Roy had decided to have a quiet dinner with his special guests. As opposed to custom, Roy was already there when the last of the dinner guests, Lya and Jake arrived. The dinner table this evening was round in contrast to the long one they had been eating at. Roy sat with Jemma to his left, beside her was Sam, beside him was Lya who sat next to Jake. There was one free place between Jake and Roy which made the guests wonder if anyone else was coming.

"Great, you are all here," said Roy with a smile once everyone was seated. "This extra chair was added by mistake, we are not waiting for anyone," he said realizing everyone's eyes were darting towards it. Then he turned to Jake and loudly whispered, "Did she say yes?" with a massive smile on his face as he looked at Lya's hand to see if the ring was there.

"Yes, your majesty" said Jake blushing.

"Splendid!" said Roy. "I insist we hold your wedding on the castle grounds. It's not every day that my advisor gets married," he added, still smiling.

"I was looking out of my window and saw Lya take a swing at you," said Sam.

"Then you knelt down. That was very confusing to see." Jake and Lya both laughed, and Lya then explained, "He called me to the garden to tell me something important. After accepting the offer to stay here, I thought he was going to propose," said Lya, "but then he said, '*I have always been on my own and loved it, never wanted kids or a wife, so let me be clear.*' This is when I tried to punch him. But then he continued saying that '*the only woman that could change my mind is the one in front of me and I humbly ask if she would have me for life and keep me that way.*' I mean who could say no to that?" Lya giggled. The group congratulated the couple and drank to their futures. Then the food arrived.

Chapter 10
A New Journey

The second sun was about to set when Sam, Lya and Jake mounted their horses to leave Vegna. Sam had packed his duffle on the back of his horse, Lya had two duffle bags on hers and Jake had three.

"What do you have in there?" Jemma asked Jake as she stood by Roy who had also come to see them off.

"One bag is mine, and two are for Lya," Jake answered. "They are things for the tavern. I plan to give it to my cousin Serma. And I had bought a few things here to take there anyway."

"We better be off," said Sam as he nudged his horse. "We will be back within a month," he said as his horse moved forward followed by Lya and Jake. As they passed through the second gate of Vegna, Sam saw Scarlett on the side of the road talking to another lady, "Goodbye Ms. Scarlett," said Sam. "Off to the free tribes, I hope to see you when I come back."

"Goodbye Sam," she answered. "Y'all be good now. You hear?" And waved to them before going back to her discussion with the other lady.

"Sweet lady," said Jake.

"A bit weird," said Lya.

"Completely nuts," said Sam, "...but that's her charm," he added. The trio laughed and continued on their journey to the gate.

Once there, Ben was on guard again, "Leaving us already?" he asked looking at Jake. "We didn't have our beer yet," he added turning towards Sam.

"We will be back in about a month," said Sam. "I promise to have a beer with you then."

"I will hold you to that," called out Ben as they passed. As soon as they crossed the gates of Vegna, the desert heat washed over them like flames from a dragon's breath.

They traveled in silence for most of the night, listening for wolves. But the desert was quiet and still. As they neared to the resting place, the horses started getting jittery and would hop to different sides every few steps. It was half-moon, so they could not see what was bothering the horses so much. Sam suggested they let the horses trot, maybe the sand was too hot for their hoofs, but Jake reminded him that the sand cools down quickly in the night. The horses started hopping from side to side even more, and this time they could hear light cracking sounds with each step. Sam remembered the picture of the scorpion on the map and told Jake and Jemma to get their horses to gallop to the resting place. Jake wanted to know the reason and lit a flint only to see a bed of scorpions on the ground.

"Hiiyaa," yelled Jake sending his horse into a gallop which was a move both Sam and Lya copied. A few minutes later, they were at the resting place. Sam's horse was limping and had a swollen leg.

"Please check my horse," Sam called to the stable hand. The short man walked over and examined the leg. He turned to Sam saying, "It's a scorpion bite. But from what I see, the horse is not feverish, he should be fine."

Sam checked the swelling as well and turned to the stable hand asking, "It's almost shafaq, do you have a place to keep the horses cool? We plan to leave by nightfall." "Yes, we do," answered the stable hand. "And he will be just fine by nightfall; rested and healed."

Sam, Jake and Lya walked into the resting place where they were immediately recognized by the manager.

"Welcome back. Do you want the same rooms? Oh, where is the other lady, the one with purple eyes?" the manager asked.

"We left her in Vegna," answered Jake. "And yes, the same rooms, please." With that, Sam took their leave and went straight to his room. As the room was underground, the only light there was from candles and lanterns, but it was refreshingly cool in comparison to the heat outside. Sam took out the map and looked at it under the light of a lantern. He checked where they saw the scorpions and wondered if they had passed the same spot on the way to Vegna or was there another way. He then traced the path with his fingers to the journey ahead and guessed the time it would take to get there, find out what he needs and return in time for Jemma's wedding. This turned his mind to Jemma, Sam wondered how he thought of her as a true and real friend when he did not even know her a month ago.

Funny how you find a connection with a total stranger, and you immediately trust them, he thought to himself, being careful not to confuse trust and friendship with romantic inclinations. Thinking that he thinks too much, Sam decided to sleep early to get an early start the next day.

Jake stood there as his father was lying in bed struck by the fever. He wanted to help but could do nothing about it. He had gotten a cloth with water to dab his father's forehead, but the slightest touch caused unbelievable pain to his father, so he just stood there. Then his father spoke, "Kahl my boy, I am not long for this world," he said, "but before I go, you need to know your truth. We hail from a tribe that was eradicated by its enemies. We were warriors with no compare, so we forged no alliances and attacked whoever we wanted to. When our enemies banded together, they became too strong, even for us. They attacked us together and, in one day, the tribe was gone. My brother, friends, relatives, all dead in one day. Very few survived. We do not know who they are, nor do we know where they are. For your sake, do not make enemies. I do not want to see you in the afterlife as a young man. I feel my time has come, I cast this body as a man proud of his son." He took a deep breath and breathed out his last. Tears welled up in Jakes eyes and his breath become short.

Jake turned in his bed and the tear that ran down the side of his cheek woke him up. It was a hard memory to keep, he thought to himself. He thought if his father was proud then, how disappointed he would be with what Jake had done so far with his life. Then he smiled again thinking how proud he would be to know his son was offered a position as the consultant for the King of Vegna and that in a room nearby slept the woman that would bear his grandchildren. This quick change in mood energized Jake and convinced him it was almost sundown. He got up from his bed, washed the sleep away and left the room for the main hall. When he got there,

93

Sam was already there eating at a table, and Lya was coming down the stairs near him. He held Lya's hand, and they both walked over to Sam.

"How is your horse?" Lya asked.

"Seems he made it," said Sam with his mouth full. "He is of good stock, it will take more than a scorpion to get him down," he added proudly. Jake and Lya joined Sam for dinner and planned their rout to Sanctuary. They checked the map for the shortest route and saw they could save a few hours of travel if they took the path showing the lone tree. After their meal, they set their horses and started their journey.

They had been riding for a few hours when Sam signaled to them to stop using only his hands. No sound was made. Jake and Lya peered into the night but could not see anything. Sam jumped from the saddle and landed lightly and silently on the desert sand. He took a few steps forward and then raised his right hand, a blue flash appeared in his hand and Sam swung the axe, immediately decapitating two bandits hiding in waiting. Sam turned towards Jake and Lya to signal that it is all clear only to see a green light pass inches from his head and thud into the third bandit behind him. The bandit groaned as he toppled forward with the green arrow shimmering from existence.

"Now they are all dead," said Jake, feeling extra proud to have contributed to the fight and doing this in front of Lya. Sam nodded and walked back to his horse, mounted it and the three continued their journey.

"Is that how your encounters with bandits look like?" asked Lya. "A swing and a swoosh and it's over? How do people fear them if they are so weak?" she continued. Jake was embarrassed by how she belittled their skills but when he

94

heard Sam laughing out loud and saw Lya burst into laughter, he realized she was only joking to which he reacted by joining the laughter.

--

Serma was a tall beautiful woman, her skin was milk white, her hair was jet black and she had red full lips and dark green eyes. She was sweeping the tavern, getting it ready for the re-opening. The chairs and tables Lya had ordered had arrived the previous night and were now in place. She was concerned that the barrels of ale might not be enough for the night as the whole town was looking forward to their favorite tavern re-opening. The musical band she had hired had been successful in many other towns and Serma was sure they would do a great job. As she was deep in thought, the tavern door opened and in walked the band she was thinking of.

"What a coincidence!" she said. "I was just thinking if you were going to practice here."

"We don't believe in coincidences," said the blond short man who was first in. "We believe in destiny."

"Stop your nonsense," replied the tall bald one. "We need to practice, and this is the best place." He said, turning to Serma.

"Do you mind?" he ended.

"Not at all," she replied. "It would be a pleasure to listen to you while I set up." With that, the last of the three men came towards Serma, took her hand and kissed it. Serma blushed. The band started tuning their instruments while Serma was finishing tidying up. Then the band started playing a sad old folk song. The song was about a girl whose husband went to war and she waited for him every day by the town's gate until he finally returned. But they were both old then and they didn't recognize each other. When the song was halfway through, the tavern door flung open and in walked Lya singing the tune to perfection with her velvet voice. Serma jumped out of her skin and when she realized it was Lya, she ran and hugged her tight. Sam and Jake followed Lya into the tavern. "We are not open yet," Serma said not knowing who Sam and Jake were.

"Serma," said Lya, "this is Jake. We will be married soon," she added showing her the ring.

"And this is Sam," continued Lya, "he is a friend and a supreme warrior." Serma looked at Jake and smiled, and then looked at Sam and her smile widened.

"Nice to meet you," said Jake.

"Yeah. Same here," said Sam feeling flustered at the beautiful woman's added smile.

The tavern's opening night was a roaring success, the customers loved the new band and Lya's performance was flawless. By the time the last person left the tavern, Sam and Jake were completely drunk. They had their arms around each other's shoulders and were singing two different songs at the same time! Lya and Serma were also exhausted but sat there and watched Sam and Jake destroy a few songs. After a while, Jake sat down to rest and passed out immediately. Sam on the other hand wanted to sing some more, but it was late, and he was not a good singer. Lya woke Jake up and led him by the hand to his room while Serma was trying her best to get Sam to stop singing and go to his room. Eventually, Serma held Sam's hand and softly said, "follow me," to which he went completely silent and followed her upstairs. She led him to his room, told him to lie down, which he did and then left, to which his only objection was a soft snore. Morning came and went, with both Sam and Jake in deep sleep. By early afternoon, both of them walked down to the tavern holding their heads. Lya and Serma had cleaned up the place, getting ready for the evening. Sam sat at the table and Jake plopped next to him. Lya came over and asked, "Are you boys okay?" in a voice a little louder than her usual tone. Sam and Jake winced at the pain. Lya laughed at their reaction and turned to Serma who had prepared bacon sandwiches and Banana milkshakes for them to alleviate the effect of the hangover. Both Jake and Sam ate their sandwiches and drank the shakes in silence. Then Sam broke the silence looking at Jake saying, "We leave at first light. Go back to bed!" And with that, both men got up and walked upstairs to their rooms to sleep again.

After a dreamless night, Sam woke up early just before the shafaq. He was feeling a lot better than the previous day and the hangover. He got up, washed his face, and got dressed. He felt very hungry and decided to have a heavy breakfast before starting his journey with Jake. Sam packed his duffle bag and walked out of the room making one final sweep to make sure nothing was forgotten. As he scanned the room, he noticed that the small tail-lace had fallen from his duffle bag and was in on the floor in the center of the room. He walked over, picked it up and tucked it in the side pocket of his duffle bag and secured it in by tightening the laces of the pocket. Sam left the room and walked downstairs where Jake was sitting in a corner with Lya, holding hands and whispering to each other and giggling. Sam walked over to the nearest table to sit down hoping not to disturb them. Jake saw him and waved for him to join them. When Sam got to Jake and Lya, he noticed that Jake's duffle back was already packed and next to him.

"Are you okay to ride?" Jake asked Sam.

"Ready and able," Sam answered, "but hungry. Can we eat before we leave?" he asked sarcastically.

"Breakfast is ready," said Lya, "Serma is bringing it out now." As Lya finished her sentence, Serma walked over with a large tray and placed it on the table, pulled up a chair and joined the trio. The tray had cured ham, an assortment of cheese, scrambled eggs, boiled eggs, Oatmeal, and fruits on it, each on a different plate. Sam was so hungry; he ate some of each. When they were finally full, Sam got up and looked at Jake, "Time to go," he said. Jake got up and both men walked outside to the horses. They set their duffle bags at the back end of the saddles and turned to say goodbye to Lya and Serma. Lya wrapped her arms around Jake's neck and kissed him deeply and said with a smile, "You better come back safely, or I will hunt you down."

Jake smiled and kissed her back, "I would not have it any other way," he said. Sam put his hand forward towards Serma to shake her hand, but Jake pushed him slightly from behind as a joke, so he put both hands up and stumbled towards Serma who welcomed him with open arms and hugged him goodbye. Then she pulled her head back and kissed Sam lightly on the lips. Sam's heart started pounding instantly as he kissed her back. Serma then said, "Come back and tell me who you are." Sam smiled and said, "And I would love to know all about you too." With that Sam and Jake mounted their horses and started towards Kiaff.

Chapter 11
To Kiaff and Beyond

While riding, Sam could not stop thinking about Serma and the kiss they shared. He did not remember ever being kissed this way before, this was the first and only kiss he remembered. Her image was stuck in his head, and he couldn't get her out of it. He tried to imagine what this kiss could lead to but was unable to focus. Without focusing on the path ahead, Sam did not notice when they entered the forest, but his attention snapped into focus when a purple blur whizzed by them, circled them twice and then whizzed away.

"It must be looking for Jemma," Jake said.

Sam did not answer but tried to keep his focus on the path. He looked around for any signs of trouble and tried to remember on the map if there was a shortcut and where it was. A short while later, his curiosity got the best of him and asked Jake to stop so they could check the map. As they checked the map, they saw that if they turned a few degrees to the right, they will be going straight to Kiaff, but will have to cross a river twice. There were no warning images by the river, so they thought a faster route would be better. They both mounted their horses and continued their journey, with a few degrees to the right. The day went by with no incidents or excitement which raised Sam's spirits that the map could be a reliable guide. But by nightfall, they found a clearing and set up camp. The fire burnt slowly which meant neither of them had to go look for firewood and the food Lya had packed for them was very satisfying. Once a fresh pair of logs was set on the fire, both Sam and Jake lied down to sleep.

Sam woke up to the sound of rustling in the bushes a few meters away. He got up and was getting ready to summon the axe when a small purple bunny hopped into view. It was still dark, so Sam knew this rabbit was at its most vulnerable. The rabbit looked at Sam and then hopped nearer. Sam was surprised at the rabbit and did not move. Then the rabbit hopped a bit closer, and Sam could see a large thorn nestled deep in the rabbit's thigh. Sam knelt down and slowly reached out, grabbed the thorn and quickly yanked it free. The rabbit let out a high-pitched shriek but did not run away. Instead, it sat there and stared at Sam. Sam sat there and stared back. A series of images suddenly went through Sam's mind as if projected in there. Sam did not understand them. Then the rabbit hopped away, and Sam lay back trying to understand what happened and finally fell asleep. By the time shafaq was starting, Sam woke up, poked the coals in the fire and started making coffee. Jake woke up to the smell of the brew, rubbed his eyes and sat where he slept. As Sam poured the coffee for him and Jake, Jake pulled out a bundle from his bag and placed it on the floor between him and Sam. In the bundle was some bread, cheese, and dried meat. The two men ate breakfast and packed up for the second day of their journey.

A couple of hours later, they got to the first point where they needed to cross the river. It was a slow river and shallow. They crossed it with ease. When they got to the other side, they saw an old man sitting on a large rock. "Hello, Sam and Jake," said the old man while he still had their back to them. "Are you on your way to the free tribes?" he asked in a rhetorical tone.

"How did you know?" asked Jake as they turned to see it was the same old man, they met on their way out of Kiaff a short while back.

"I told you; I know what was, what is and what might be. And you might be going to the free tribes."

"We left our friend with you when we passed here the last time, where is he now?" asked Jake, looking around for Moro.

"He has long gone," said Blandi. "Moro had lost himself when he joined me, then he found himself and left."

"How did he find himself?" asked Sam.

"Oh, wouldn't you like to know, Sam?" answered Blandi. Then he added, "Moro had a troubled soul. He worked through his issues and found peace. And once he found this peace, he wanted to share it with the world. So, he up and left to travel the world and spread whatever wisdom he found."

"Well, good for him," said Jake, "Moro was a good man stuck in bad deeds. Now he will be good through and through."

"Thank you, old man," said Sam and started to leave when Blandi said, "Be well, Sam, your future is unwritten, and you hold the quill. Write it well." With that Jake and Sam left Blandi on their way to Kiaff.

By sunset, Sam and Jake had reached the second river to cross. This one was deep and wide and there was no way in sight to cross the river. While the horses were drinking, Sam and Jake decided to check the Map for a clue as to where and how they could cross. They unwrapped the leather map and started tracing their journey.

"That's the tree in the desert," said Jake, "and this is where we met the old man," he added pointing to the locations on the map.

"But where is the rock which shows us where to pass here?" said Sam. They looked around and there was no rock in sight. Sam looked back at the map and saw a mark on it that looked like a snake, he had thought it was a scribble before. The mark was a little bit to the left of the red line on the map that signified the path.

"Hey Jake," said Sam, "look here, do you see the snake? If we are to the left of the crossing, we might end up near it." Sam had not finished his sentence when both horses reared and started kicking wildly. Then the horses took off at a sprint while the two men stood there trying to figure out what happened.

"What the hell," called Jake with a green bow materializing in his hand, but he did not notch an arrow or even look for one. A giant anaconda came out of the water, lifted its head and stared down at the two men. Sam felt the weight of the axe in his hand. The snake snapped at them, making loud hissing sounds. It was a fight or flight situation, and with the horses gone, they thought they had only the first option. Sam swung his axe and ran at the snake, but its tail found him midway and threw him back to where he started. Jake notched an arrow and fired, but the arrow disappeared before it got to the snake. Sam got up and charged again only to repeat the result of the previous try and the same happened to Jake's second try. A purple blur whizzed by the two men and went through the snake's tail. The snake recoiled with pain and started writhing. Sam and Jake got worried that the rabbit might have been stuck in the snake's tough skin, but their concerns were alleviated when the rabbit whizzed by and stopped near them for a split second before leaving. The snake slid into the river and swam downstream with its tail leaving a thin trail of blood in the water.

"Saved by the bunny again," said Jake, "but now we do not have horses anymore."

"You still know how to walk, right?" said Sam, "We will buy horses in Kiaff."

"With what money?" said Jake. "The coin purse is with the horses!"

"We will figure it out," said Sam, "but now, let's cross this river." The two men walked along the river until they got to a rock which was similar to the one on the map. They ventured into the river only to discover that the water was very shallow, and they could cross easily.

Sam and Jake continued their journey on foot, walking in the middle of the path to give themselves the extra nanosecond of time should a speeding furball decide to go through them. A few minutes later, they heard a woman scream in the distance. They looked at each other and ran towards the sound. As they neared, they heard a man scream in pain. When they got to a bush behind which the sound was coming from, they crept and got close to see what was going on. A man lay dead on the ground with blood flowing from his chest and another man was checking his pockets. A woman was being tied to a tree by two men. One of the men stood in front of the tied woman and ripped her shirt smiling. "Hey boys, check these out," he said pointing at her breasts. He licked his lips and turned to see the man who was checking the body also dead and above him stood two men. One had a blue axe in his hand, which was dripping blood, and the other a green bow made from what looked like light. The bandit turned to find the man who was tying the lady slumped against the tree. As he turned to face them, he saw a flash of blue near him and then the world started spinning.

The lady screamed at the sight of the bandit being beheaded by Sam's mighty axe and was worried these two men were also bandits. But when Jake cut her loose and handed her her shawl from the ground, she felt a bit safer. "Thank you, dear sirs," she said, "I am in your debt. You saved my life from these..." and she trailed off crying. "There, there," said Sam, "You are safe now."

Sam looked around for the bandit's horses and was lucky to have heard one of them snort nearby, so he didn't have to look for too long. Jake, on the other hand, went through their pockets and came out with a new bag of coins.

"This might be more profitable than honest work," Jake said with a chuckle.

"Now we have horses and coin," said Sam. "Time to move on."

"Ma'am," Sam said turning to the lady, "we are on our way to Kiaff, I am Sam, and this is Jake. If you are going our way, you are welcome to join us. If you are going in another direction, then you can have one of these horses and be on your way."

"My name is Lori, and I have just come from Kiaff. I am going to Sanctuary to visit my friend there, who owns a tavern. I will speak well of you two," she said.

"Is your friend Lya?" asked Jake with excitement.

"Yes," said Lori, "do you know her?"

"Know her?" Jake scoffed, "We are to be married upon my return!"

"Then I will tell her of this encounter, Jake, also that she is lucky to have a gentleman hero for a husband." Jake's ego swelled at the word 'hero'. He had never been called that before, all he remembered was being called thief, bandit and raider. They all mounted their new horses and went their separate ways with Sam and Jake riding to Kiaff and Lori to Sanctuary.

At the gate of Kiaff, the guards recognized one of the horses and stopped Sam.

"Where did you get this horse from?" asked the guard in an accusing tone.

"Three bandits attacked a man and woman in the forest. They killed the man, but we managed to save the lady. These are two of their horses," answered Sam, "the third horse is with the lady who is on her way to Sanctuary. Her name is Lori." The guard looked relieved.

"She is my sister and wants to visit her friends...I was worried about her, so I asked her to go with someone she knows," he said. "She chose the worst person to go to the woods with!" he added angrily, but then composed himself and said, "Thank you gentlemen, for helping Lori out. If you need anything while in Kiaff, just go to any guards' office and ask for Diapso, that's me." The two men thanked him and walked into Kiaff. As they walked in, Sam could not help but wonder how one kingdom was designed in circles and the other in squares; *there must have been a shape that is best and works for all,* he thought to himself. Then he dismissed the thought completely and he and Jake found their way to the tavern they stayed at during their previous visit.

Paul was collecting plates that his patrons had left behind and carrying them to the kitchen when he spotted a large silhouette walking through the door. His first reaction was to welcome the new guest, then he noticed it was Sam. He dropped the plates and ran into the kitchen. The clatter of the plates turned a few heads in the tavern and a waitress ran to pick them up. Sam paid no attention to the commotion and walked to an empty table and sat down with Jake trailing behind. A minute later, a waitress walked over and asked for their order. "Two beers, please," said Jake pulling a coin from his newly acquired pouch.

"Tell Paul we mean him no harm," said Sam looking into the waitresses' eyes. She could not help but stare back at his purple eyes and nod absent-mindedly. When the beer came, it was Paul bringing it. He placed the jugs on the table and turned to leave when Sam stopped him. "We mean you no harm, Paul, you can relax," said Sam. Paul swallowed hard, turned to leave when he suddenly remembered a detail he had not shared. Paul cleared his throat and said, "I forgot to mention something to you. The red-haired lady with the bow, had very unique arrows in her quilt; they were black with yellow feathers." Sam's face changed, giving Paul a near heart attack with fear. But Sam did not move, he just remembered his dream of the black arrow and yellow feathers killing his parents. He tried remembering more, such as the face, gender or hair color of the attacker, but he got nothing. One thing he knew, is, that the arrows that killed his parents came from the lady who acted as Jemma's nanny. With this thought, he drank a deep gulp of beer and shared this information with Jake. By the time they finished their third drink, both Sam and Jake were ready for a good night's sleep as the journey was to be continued the next morning. Jake had already organized their rooms and paid for them, so both Sam and Jake went upstairs for a well-earned rest.

Morning came too quickly for Sam. He was with Serma in a wonderful dream when a knock on his bedroom door woke him up. He got up and opened the door only to find a smiling Jake asking, "Breakfast?"

Sam nodded, turned back to the room where he washed his face, put on his shoes and joined Jake in the hallway to go for breakfast. Paul's menu was limited, and his food was not that good, so both men decided to have the safest bet which was oatmeal. Once they were done eating, they got up, got their duffle bags and left the tavern to continue their journey. Just before they mounted the horses, they checked the map again to make sure they took the fastest and safest route. The red line on the map went through Kiaff and out from the other side. Neither Sam nor Jake knew if there was a gate there, but the map had been too reliable up until now, so they decided to follow the red line. They got on their horses and started riding through Kiaff.

Just like in Vegna, Sam noticed that the closer they got to the center of the city where the king's castle was, the larger and fancier the houses looked. They rode in silence for most of the morning as both of them were busy looking around and taking in the scenes of the kingdom. By early afternoon, they had both become hungry and decided to stop at the next tavern for lunch. They passed long rows of houses and shops for over an hour but not a single tavern. Getting very hungry, Jake decided to ask for directions and stopped a passerby to ask him where the closest tavern was. The man looked at them carefully for a minute and then pointed in the direction they were already going. They looked at each other and kept moving. On the right of the cobbled street, behind a sign for a shop, was a sign for a food outlet, but it had no door. Sam dismounted and walked to the window nearby which was open, and a pretty lady sat at looking out.

"Excuse me, miss," Sam said, "can you tell me where the tavern is?"

The lady in the window then answered, "You must be new here. We do not have taverns in this area of Kiaff, we have outlets like this one where you ask for your food, we make it and give it to you, then you go eat it at home."

Sam and Jake looked at each other in surprise. This was a new concept to them, but being hungry, they ordered wraps and decided to eat them as they rode. A few minutes later, the lady came back with their food, and they continued the journey eating on horseback. A while later, they saw that the houses were getting smaller and more run down.

"We must be getting far away from the center," Jake said. Sam nodded in agreement. By late afternoon, the scenery had completely changed and all around them were large fields of crops.

"This must be their agricultural section," said Sam, looking around at the wide spaces and the mountain that had appeared in the horizon. "And this is on our path," said Jake, pointing to the mountain. They kept riding in silence until they saw a large building by the end wall. As they approached it, they saw that it looked like an inn. They got to the door, dismounted and walked inside. The place was empty save for an old man sitting in a chair who was startled by the two.

"How can I help you?" he asked.

"We want lodging for the night and to go through the gate in the morning," answered Sam.

"This is not a place for lodging, young man," answered the old timer, "This is the guard's house, and you came between shifts, so it's empty for the next few minutes. I suggest you find somewhere else to stay." The old man's tone was very harsh and lacked all forms of hospitality which led the travelers to believe him. Just then they heard people speaking outside and then a few guards walked through the door. They stood there staring at the two new arrivals. Jake then remembered the guard at the other gate and said, "We are friends of Diapso."

One of the guards then said, "From the other gate? Great guy. Why did he send you here? Is Lori OK?" his voice sounded very concerned.

"Lori is fine and on her way to Sanctuary to see Lya, my fiancé." said Jake, "And Diapso is fine too, but he did tell us to go to the guard's house and ask for him if we needed anything. So here we are. We just need lodging for the night and passage through the gate as we plan to go to the free tribes in the morning."

"Any friend of Diapso is a friend of mine," said another guard and the rest joined in with 'same here' and 'me too'. "Then it's settled. You two will stay here for the night and they will escort you through the gate in the morning," said the old man nodding towards the guards.

The night with the guards was fun and filled with laughter, even when Jake told them about their encounter with the bandits and Lori's rescue. The guards were friendly and welcomed having new people visit with news from the kingdom and the outside world. Sam and Jake ate and drank with the guards until it was time for them to retire to the rooms the guards had set aside for them. The two visitors went to their rooms and slept dreamlessly. By sunrise, the guards sounded the morning bugle which woke Sam and Jake up as well. They washed their faces and went out of their rooms to join the guards in the mess hall. Breakfast was already prepared, and they ate scrambled eggs and bacon with the guards. After breakfast, the old man announced it was "shift change" and the guards filed out of the door followed by Sam and Jake. They all mounted their horses and started towards the gate. Once there, the guards officially relieved the other shift and took their posts. A few minutes later, Sam and Jake were out of the gate and on their way to the snow-capped mountains leading to the free tribes.

Chapter 12
The Mountain

About an hour after leaving the gate, the ground started sloping upwards and became rocky. As the horses walked up the path, they stumbled a few times as they would step on loose rocks and stones which had rolled onto the path due to snow, rain and wind. Sam and Jake decided to walk with the horses as opposed to riding them to ensure their safety. The road got steeper by the minute and Sam and Jake made sure to kick stones off the path to keep the horses safe. As they ascended, the temperature started dropping as if a degree with each step. After a while, Jake got very cold and reached into his duffle bag and pulled out a heavy Jacket. Sam pulled out a leather jacket that was lined with sheep's wool and put in on. Both men were warm now. As they moved higher and higher into the mountain, they started seeing small patches of snow on the side of the path by the bushes. They felt like they were halfway there, until they looked up to see they were far from being halfway there. The horses were now getting cold, and their breath came out in plumes of smoke. Sam and Jake reached into their duffle bags and pulled out their blankets which they put on the horses.

As the day went by, Sam and Jake walked the road with the horses in tow. By late afternoon, Sam turned to Jake and said, "We need to check the map if there is a cave somewhere here for us to stay the night. It's way colder than I expected, and I doubt we can sleep outside." As he finished speaking, they heard a howling sound in the distance. But it did not sound like wolves howling. Hearing the sound Jake rushed near Sam who was unfolding the map to see if they were on the right track.

"Huh. Funny," said Sam, "The red line usually skirts the drawn animals but this one goes through that one." Pointing at what looked like a giant dog or wolf. "I guess there is no other path!" said Jake. They examined the map further to see that there was a cave further up the mountain, but it was still a while away.

"Maybe if we ride at a trot or gallop, we can get there before nightfall," said Jake. Sam agreed and both men got back on their horses and started at a trot. Sam was an accomplished rider and looked steady in the saddle at a trot, Jake was a good racer but bad trotter, he was bouncing on the horse with an "umph" at each step. A few minutes later, they heard the howling from behind them and decided that it would be safer to gallop as they should be getting closer to the cave.

"Battling these creatures at the mouth of the cave is safer than in the open," said Sam. "This way, they cannot attack from behind."

"So—ouonds li—ke a good ide—a," answered Jake as they slowed down to a trot. Sam looked ahead and saw the mouth of the cave. By now, the entire ground and walls were covered in Ice and snow, which raised Sam's concern about the horses slipping. He dismounted and slowly led the horse to the mouth of the cave while constantly looking inside to see if there were any animals there. It was getting dark, and he could not see deep enough into the cave. Jake, who was trailing behind also got off this horse and walked to Sam saying, "This should help," and produced a stick on which he had wrapped a piece of cloth and in his other hand he had a flint. A few tries of the flint and the makeshift torch was alight.

Sam walked into the cave first with the light and was followed by Jake. They had walked about 50 meters into the cave until they reached the wall signaling the end of the cave. But the wall was made of ice and not rock.

"This must have been a waterfall of some kind," said Jake. Sam simply turned back to the entrance and sat on one of the rocks that were scattered there.

"We need to get wood and start a fire, otherwise we will all freeze to death," said Jake, motioning to Sam to get up and help. Both men went out of the cave and started looking around for firewood. Jake went left and Sam went right. A few seconds later, Sam heard Jake calling him and ran towards him. Jake had found a large deposit of firewood, as if prepared for the travelers who visit the cave and needed Sam's help to carry enough for the night. "I don't know who set these out here, but I thank them," said Jake as he carried his haul of logs. Sam, carrying double of what Jake was carrying simply answered with a "uh hum." Back at the cave, the men got the fire started and reached into their bags to see what food they can have that evening. None of the food with them required cooking, which was a pleasant surprise since they were worried the smell would attract the howling beasts. After they ate, Jake produced a small ornate metal flask, took a sip of it and offered it to Sam.

"What's in it?" asked Sam, feeling doubtful.

"Oh, just something to warm up our blood so that it does not freeze in the night," answered Jake with a wink. Sam took a sip and felt the fire start from his mouth down to his throat. He swallowed what was in his mouth but fell into a coughing fit, with Jake laughing hysterically. "That'll put hair on your chest," said Sam as he regained his breath.

"It sure will," laughed Jake.

Suddenly, they heard a growl at the mouth of the cave, and then sounds of scuttling paws. The horses were quiet and not restless, which confused Sam and Jake alike. From the darkness of the exterior, a giant head came into the light. It was that of an unusually giant wolf that had the top half of its fur grey and the bottom half white. The wolf's eyes were piercing purple and its fangs larger than a man's hand. Both men stood still, trying to summon their weapons but neither had any luck. The wolf had now entered the cave and was standing almost at Sam's height while growling at them. Sam and Jake wanted to fight or run, but they got completely paralyzed while the slow-moving wolf walked from left to right and back staring at them. Then the wolf staired straight into Sam's eyes, who stared back. A couple of seconds later, the wolf's expression changed from dangerous to house pet. And then sat on its hind legs, wagged its tail with its mouth open and tongue dangling to the side.

"What happened?" asked Jake.

"I don't know," answered Sam. "He seems to have changed personalities! Do animals get that too?" he asked Jake back. Neither of the men dared move and the wolfdog

114

just sat there waging its tail. Eventually, Sam braved taking a step closer to the beast, hoping it will stay there but the animal lowered its head and got it closer to Sam's face and licked it. Sam was completely shocked and at the same time overwhelmed by the wolfdog's action. He put his hand out and the animal got closer and rubbed its head against Sam, starting with his hand and almost covering Sam's complete upper half from the waist. What puzzled the men further was that the horses seemed not to be bothered by the animal which signified that it was not being aggressive. After a while, the wolfdog and the men had gotten used to each other's presence and the men decided to sleep hoping the animal stays on guard. They lay their blankets and lied down to sleep only to have the beast walk up to where Sam was sleeping and curl up beside him. But the animal was so large, it ended up wrapping around Sam.

Sam woke up refreshed after a deep sleep, feeling very warm. As he got up, the animal got up too and walked outside the cave where it stretched and yawned. It then walked to the right of the cave where it found a puddle from which it drank. Sam followed it outside and collected snow and Ice into the coffee pot which he then placed on the coals from last night's fire. It was shafaq and Sam was completely taken by the reflection of the orange light on the snow around him. It looked like light emitted from every spot on the mountain.

What a magnificent view, Sam thought to himself as he looked back into the cave to check on the coffee. Jake woke up to the movement and the smell of coffee. He looked like he had a rough night dealing with the cold. Sam poured Jake a cup and himself one and they sipped their coffee in silence. Once they had drank their coffee, the men packed and led the horses outside the cave to continue their journey. The wolfdog was waiting there with its purple eyes darting from the horses to Sam and to Jake. The men checked the map one more time and figured out the way to go. They mounted their steeds and rode in that direction.

By midday, the sun was shining brightly and as opposed to the previous day, the ice and snow reflected the sun's heat making both Sam and Jake feel comfortably warm without the need for a jacket. The wolfdog was walking the trail with them as they traversed the mountain routes. They had gotten used to having it with them and every once in a while, Sam would reach out and pet the beast whose tail would wag at the event. Suddenly, the beast's ears popped up and his hackles stood on end. The beast growled softly while it looked straight ahead. Sam and Jake dismounted and walked by the animal as it slowly moved toward what was bothering it. Without even trying, both Sam and Jake felt the weight of their weapons in their hands.

Suddenly, from under the snow a giant white cat-like animal jumped at the trio. Sam's axe sung, Jake's bolt was fired, and the Wolfdog leapt to meet it. The beasts scuffled for a bit and then moved away from each other with the wolfdog growling and what looked like a sabretooth...hissing. Jake fired another arrow into the sabretooth, and it winced at the pain but did not take its eyes off the wolfdog. Seeing that it is clearly distracted, Sam slowly walked within reach of the sabretooth and swung his mighty axe at it. The axe missed the animal completely as it had seen Sam move and had jumped to the side at the exact moment he swung. That sudden movement triggered an attack by the wolfdog who had managed to catch the sabretooth by the neck and was choking it to submission. The giant cat struggled to get away, but the wolfdog had a firm jaw grip on it. A few seconds later, the giant cat was still. The wolfdog let go of its neck and walked over to Sam who saw a couple of claw marks on its muzzle. Sam grabbed some snow and rubbed it on the wolfdog's wounds while petting the other side of its face. Jake walked over to the sabretooth thinking of taking its fur when he noticed the animal was still alive.

"It's still alive," Jake called to Sam.

"Great," said Sam. "It would be a shame for such a beast to die. It's a beast of myth. Let's leave before it regains its strength." And the men mounted their horses and trotted on. After a few hours, they had reached the part of the mountain where the rest of their journey was downhill. Fearing for the horses slipping, they dismounted and walked along the frozen path with the wolfdog walking beside Sam. As they traveled lower and lower, they could feel the temperature rise again and the snow-covered land was now clear, with small patches of snow on the sides of the path.

By sundown, they had reached flat ground again and were walking in a forest lush with greenery. They were looking for a clearing to camp when the wolfdog suddenly bolted from near them and disappeared into the forest. Jake who was ahead called Sam to tell him he had found a clearing. Sam walked over with his horse and tethered it next to Jake's. They collected firewood and started a fire. A few minutes later, the wolfdog came into the camp carrying a dear in its mouth. It dropped the dear by the fire and laid on the ground by Sam.

"Well, this is a surprise," said Jake, "Your giant dog is bringing us food!" while he pulled out his knife and started skinning and cutting the animal. Sam and Jake had their fill, and the wolfdog had the rest. By the time they were going to sleep, there was hardly anything left of the deer besides one final bone which the wolfdog was chewing on.

"Since this animal is now clearly your friend, do you want to give him a name?" asked Jake.

Sam thought for a while and said, "I want to give him a strong name. A name that would make people think twice about messing with him." Then he fell silent for a moment. "Zeus," Sam called out suddenly, waking Jake from the edge of sleep giving him a fright that he got up in a fighting stance. "I shall call him Zeus," said Sam. At hearing his new name, Zeus who had just finished eating the last bone, walked over to where Sam was, lay next to him and went almost immediately to sleep. Sam closed his eyes and slept.

Sam was in a forest, running...with pain searing through his right leg. He looked down to see the blood still running down his leg. He had to get to the healer in the village. When he got to the edge of the village, he hid behind a bush and peeked out from it to see the village was on fire and everyone outside dead. He heard a rustling in the bush behind him to see a man carrying a child and holding a woman's hand and running from the village. On the opposite side of the village, he saw a man with auburn hair carrying a large axe and walk into the forest, disappearing behind the greenery. Sam walked into the village and looked around to see if the healer was still there. Then he spotted him lying on the ground. Sam ran to the healer to check if he was dead only to discover he was on his last breath. Seeing the cut on Sam's leg the healer said two words, "blue ointment," while looking at Sam's cut and then was no more. Sam got up and walked towards the

healer's house looking for the blue ointment. The house had
just caught fire and Sam had little time to find the medicine.
Being only five years old, Sam could not see the shelves, so he
stood on the table in the middle of the large room and looked
around to see the shelves. He found the blue ointment, jumped
off the table, crashing into the ground as his leg could not
carry him. He staggered to get up, but dragged himself to the
shelves, reached out with his hand and grabbed the glass jar
with the blue ointment and got out of the house as fast as he
could as the flames were engulfing it. He opened the jar and
grabbed the ointment to rub on the wound on his right leg.
The ointment felt fleshy with sharp edges.

Sam woke up startled with his hand in Zeus's mouth. Zeus
on the other hand had not bit nor moved as Sam had put his
hand in his mouth. Sam then wiped his hand from Zeus' saliva
on his leggings and felt the scar on his leg through his clothes.
Seeing it was almost shafaq, Sam decided that he had had
enough sleep and it was time for him to wake up. He poured
some water from his canteen into the pot and placed it on the
coals from last night's fire. A few minutes later, the aroma of
coffee filled the air waking both Jake and Zeus up. Jake
stretched while still laying down, but Zeus got up and
stretched with a massive yawn. Sam had put some water out
for Zeus who lapped it all up. They were still engorged from
the previous night's meal, so they decided to skip breakfast
and head to the free tribes as early as possible. They packed
camp and mounted their steeds and started towards the free
tribes with Zeus walking by Sam's horse. They took the path
towards the free tribes with the hopes of getting there before
midday. As they traveled the path, they noticed the complete

lack of sounds in these forests, no birds, not squirrels or other forest dwelling creatures. "I have never been here before," said Jake, "but should a forest be so quiet?"

Sam turned to him and said, "I have no clue, I can't remember ever being here." Then they heard a loud shriek in the sky. They looked up to see a massive eagle circling overhead. Jake turned to Sam and said, "I think the animals in this part of the land are all huge. Look at your dog for example!" Sam thought on what Jake had said and thought it might be the case. They kept their slow pace until they reached a huge wall made of tree trunks. They traced the wall until they got to a massive gate. Standing guard were two giant sentries, almost an arm taller than Sam who was considered a giant already. "Good day to you," said Jake in a friendly tone. "Is this the entrance to the free tribes?"

"Yes," answered the sentry on the right.

"May we enter?" asked Jake keeping his friendly tone. "Free tribes welcome all outsiders," said the sentry, and then looking at Sam added, "and natives." Sam felt a hint of home at this and led the way into the free tribes.

Chapter 13
Free Tribes

Expecting an elaborate entrance, Sam was very disappointed to see that the scenery did not change at all with the crossing of the gate. It was as if they were still walking in the forest. The only detail he noticed was that the path widened a bit. Sam, Jake and Zeus traveled the path in front of them which eventually led them to an opening where a small village with a few wooden houses stood. The ground between the houses was green and children played there. They walked to the center of the village and looked around hoping they would find someone who can show them where the elders were. An old man walked to them and said, "Welcome strangers. What brings you here?"

"We are trying to find someone who can tell us about the history of a specific tribe," answered Jake.

"Well, old Isaiah knows every bit of history there is to know," answered the old man, "but he is two villages in this direction," he said as he pointed to a thin path ahead.

"And how far are these villages?" asked Jake.

"Oh, about a half day's ride," said the old man. They thanked him, got on their horses and started their journey. Zeus had been standing by Sam and some children had come up to him to pet him and they surrounded him. When he saw Sam leaving, he wanted to go, but the kids blocked his path, so he stayed in spite of him. Sam then called out, "Zeus. Here boy," and Zeus jumped above the wall of kids and sped towards Sam only to slow down to their speed once he reached the horses.

They rode past the first village and made it to the second village by sundown, The village had about fifteen houses in it. The houses were made of wood and had thatch roofs. The village grounds were of grass and in the center of the village was a stone well that had a bucket tied to a rope. There were a few children playing, and many doors were open and light came from the houses. As it was supper time, almost all the houses had smoke coming from the kitchen chimneys and the smell of all this food made Sam's stomach rumble. This is when he and Jake realized they had not eaten all day and were getting very hungry. An old man was sitting by the well and they guessed it was old Isaiah. They walked over to the old man. He had bright green eyes, long white hair, and a bushy beard. When he saw them approaching, he stood up. He stood at least two hands taller than Sam and with his muscular physique looked daunting. "Good evening," said Sam, "are you Isaiah?"

The man laughed hard and said, "I wish! No boy, I am not Isaiah. He is not here at the moment, but I am. So how can I help you?" Sam thought for a moment that if this is not Isaiah, and he looks like the oldest man in the village, how old is Isaiah?

"We seek him for information," said Jake trying to be as friendly as he could with the white giant who was now petting Zeus and being playful with him.

"Well, he is not here. He will be gone for a while. But as I said, I am here," said the man. "How can I help you?"

"We need to know about a tribe that lived in these parts many years ago but are no longer there," said Sam thinking this might either start the conversation or end it. The old man stopped playing with Zeus and looked Sam dead in the eye for a few seconds and then said, "I cannot help you. The only one who knows about them is Isaiah as he is the last of them. But he is gone."

"Do you know where he went?" asked Jake hoping that the answer was to the next village. "To his birthplace," answered the old man, and then added, "over the river where the tribe actually lived. But heed my warning, very few can cross the river, it is meant for the few that come from there." He warned.

A tall, strong and stout woman stepped out of one of the houses and walked towards the men talking, "Abram, it's dinner time," she said from a short distance. When she got there, Zeus came close to sniff her and she quickly said, "*wisht,*" to him, making him jump back and cower behind Sam. Zeus's reaction surprised Sam and Jake, and the old man turned to her and said, "He is a cute dog, why be mean to him?"

"My hands smell of meat and he would expect a treat. I have no time for dogs. Now come on in and have dinner." Then she turned to Sam and Jake adding, "You two as well. There is enough food." Being hungry, both of them walked behind her with Zeus trailing behind.

Dinner was amazing. Neither Sam nor Jake had ever tasted something so delicious, and Zeus got some leftovers which were given to him to eat by the house door. "I don't

123

like having dogs in the house," the lady had said. "He can guard the door though." After dinner, Sam shared his story with Abram and his wife, but they had very limited information to add to what he already knew. He showed them the tail-lace and the only thing they confirmed was that it would have belonged to a baby that had a chief or King as a father, and the fact that it bore the bear insignia meant that it came from the disappearing tribe. Sam asked them if they know of the lady with the black arrows and yellow feathers, but the old couple said they knew nothing about it. They had lived in that village their whole life and did not get involved in things that were from outside their boundaries.

When the moon was almost in the middle of the sky, Sam and Jake took their leave from the old couple who refused to let them leave in the night. "We would be the laughingstock of the village if we turn away guests in the middle of the night," said Abram. "You will stay here even if I have to tie you up and gag you," he added. Both Sam and Jake knew he was not joking as the look on his face was very serious. So, they accepted the couple's hospitality for the night. As the house was made of one large room, they wondered which corner would be theirs when the lady pointed them at their beds which were in a hidden loft above the fireplace. "These are what we call winter-beds," she said. "They stay warm in the night because the fireplace is beneath them. Tonight is a cool night and we put out the fire early to make sure you are not too hot, but also to keep you from getting cold in the night."

"Thank you very much," said Jake. "You are very kind and hospitable indeed." With that Sam and Jake climbed the

124

ladder to their lofty beds and lay down. Sleep came quickly to both of them.

In the morning when everyone was awake and having coffee, there was a loud knock at the door. The old man opened the door to reveal a tall thin man with a grey-haired woman.

"Welcome, Chief," said the old man as he moved away from the door, allowing the couple to move in. The tall man walked in looking around and said, "I heard we have visitors here. And when they stay at the village elder's house, you know they are important," ending with a fake smile. Sam did not feel easy towards this man but kept his face emotionless. "Yes," said the old man, "they came looking for Isaiah and stayed the night with us as it was getting late. Here let me introduce you. Sam and Jake, this is Gobon, our new chief." Gobon was not happy with the word 'new' but said nothing. The grey-haired woman that was with Gobon who was silent the whole time looked at Sam and said, "You have interesting eyes, my boy. Are you from around here?"

Sam was not sure why she would ask and did not know, "I am not sure, ma'am. I have lost a lot of my memory," he replied honestly. She smiled and nodded a thank you and then stood still and silent.

"So, what do you want from Isaiah?" asked Gobon, "Almost no one from the outside asks for him." Sam was about to answer when Jake tapped his foot against Sam's, signaling that something was afoot and then answered, "We heard that he could help us train Zeus, the dog you saw outside."

"Ah yes, it is rare to see a tame one of those. From what I know, only five have ever had masters. But it is a well-known fact that once they have a master, they become very tame and friendly as long as their master is calm."

"Then you better hold your temper, buddy," said Jake to Sam with a slight laugh.

"We shall keep you no longer," said Gobon and walked out of the door followed by the grey-haired woman. After they left, the old man and woman turned to each other and to Sam and Jake and came close to speak in whispers. "You need to leave quickly," said the old man. "Gobon got his position when the old chief was killed, as Gobon was his right-hand man. And they were both vile and deceitful. And that grey-haired woman with him was with the old chief as well. What a horrible creature she is." The old woman leaned in, adding, "The only good thing about this group is the girl they raised. With all their poison, they could not darken her heart. A good woman if I say so myself. Interestingly, she has eyes like yours. We know she was not the chief's daughter, as she only appeared here when she was about three years old, but no one knew where she came from, and no one dared ask."

"Now go and travel through the forest where they cannot watch or follow you," said the old man, rushing them to leave.

After thanking the old couple, Sam and Jake got on their horses and took off in the direction of the river with Zeus at their flank. They left the path and went into the thick of the forest for a while before slowing down. They kept looking back to check if anyone was following them but could not see anyone. They continued their journey slowly as they followed the path on the map. After an hour, they had made it to a clearing in the forest, making it easier to get the horses into a trot, but then Jake's horse took off in a gallop and Sam followed him to the edge of the clearing where the forest started being thick again. There, Jake's horse stopped, Jake jumped off and the green bow was in his hand.

Sam got there and got off his horse quietly and went to Jake asking, "What's the matter?" He knew in his heart that there was real danger as Jake's bow appeared only when needed.

"Shshsh!" said Jake pointing to the opening in the clearing where they had just come from. A few seconds later, two riders, all dressed in black got out of the thick forest. "They have been following us," said Jake, "I spotted them a short while ago when we left the trail, and they followed our every turn."

"Why don't we set a trap to see if they are friend or foe," said Sam. "I will sit at the edge of the clearing and when they see me, we will see how they react."

"That would be a good Idea if they did not know we are together," said Jake, "but it is wise to distract them, so we can separate them." By then, the riders were getting closer, and Sam and Jake decided to stand on opposite sides of the entrance so as to get the riders from both sides. As the two riders went through the first bush, both Sam and Jake said, "Hey!" to them, but each was on a different side. Each rider turned to a different side and jumped off their horses with their weapons drawn. The rider that was on Jake's side landed on the floor with a thud, dead, and a green arrow disappeared from his neck. The rider on Sam's side landed and delivered a blow which ricocheted off the sapphire axe. Zeus then jumped at the rider biting his head clean off and then dropping it at Sam's feet. Sam petted the animal's head saying, "Good boy."

Back on their horses and riding through the forest, Sam and Jake discussed Gobon and why he would chase after them like that. They had no enemies here but somehow this man made himself an enemy by simply seeing them. There must be more to this story and they both hoped Isaiah had the answers to the many new questions they have. By midday, when both suns shown high in the sky, they heard the sound of a raging river.

"We must be close," said Sam edging his horse to go faster. Within a few minutes, Sam, Jake and Zeus stood at the banks of a deep, wide and dangerous river. There was no bridge or shallow end to cross it. They stood there looking at the map to make sure they are in the right place. Once confirmed that they are in the right place, they started studying the river to find how to cross it. Their concern was that the river moved too fast and had rocks in the middle of it which can be dangerous if they try to swim through it. And their primary concern was the waterfall that the river had downstream. They sat there for a while, trying to figure it out and examining their options when Jake suddenly got up and ran up the river. Sam ran after him to see what he was up to. Jake checked the water speed and the distance and then smiled.

"Check this out," he said to Sam as he grabbed a small wooden log from the ground and threw it into the river. They both watched the log float down the river from the point Jake threw it and watched the log move across the river through the rocks while still traveling down. "You are a genius!" exclaimed Sam with excitement. With that, they went back to the horses, got what they needed and then walked back up to where Jake threw the block of wood and jumped in. Zeus, being a large dog with great jumping ability, had found a few flat rocks along the river and jumped from one to the other to arrive at the other side with the two men.

The water was ice cold, giving a shock of energy to both men. Sam tried swimming faster to the other side, but Jake called out to him to just float. Any change in speed can have him smashing into a rock. The swim took about one minute but felt like a lifetime to the freezing men. When they reached the other side, their first thought was to start a fire and dry their wet clothes while they warm their freezing bodies. About an hour later, their clothes were dry, and they were warm by the extra-large fire they built. They put out the fire, got dressed and then continued their journey on foot. They had walked for about two hours when they came upon rock ruins. From where they stood, it looked like they were in what was once a large and thriving city. There were large and cylindrical stone pillars on both sides of the entrance that were covered with a creeper. As they walked in between them, they could make out that they entered what was once a large hall but is now a few pillars standing in a forest. They walked into the space and saw a large rock throne at the end of it. On the throne was a large man with auburn hair and white streaks through his long hair and thick beard. He looked foreboding sitting on that throne. Sam walked over towards him, with Jake behind.

The man stood up and with a booming voice said, "Who are you and what are you doing in my sacred grounds?" With that, he grabbed the axe that was by the throne and lifted it to his shoulder. Zeus walked up next to Sam and stood by him growling. Jake stayed behind Sam jerking his hand to summon the bow but to no avail.

"We have come to talk to old Isaiah," answered Sam loudly. The man walked slowly towards Sam and said, "Why do you seek me, boy?" Sam then patted Zeus's head to calm him down and said, "I was told Isaiah can help me regain my memories and tell me more about who I am," as he did, he pulled the tail-lace from his pocket and lifted it so Isaiah could see it.

"Sam," whispered Isaiah, dropping the axe and walking quickly with his arms out signaling he wanted to hug Sam. Sam stood still and Isaiah grabbed him in a hug lifting him from his feet.

"Sam. Sam. Sam," Isaiah kept repeating as his voice started breaking and tears ran down his cheeks. Isaiah put Sam down and looked him over with a giant grin on his face. "You have grown into a great man," said Isaiah touching Sam's bulging muscles, then staring into Sam's purple eyes he said, "and I see your father in you." With that, he hugged Sam tightly again. Then Isaiah patted Zeus and made a hand gesture, to which Zeus reacted by lying down. Isaiah walked over to Jake and put his hand out for a handshake. Jake's hand met Isaiah's with a firm shake and said, "Kahl." Isaiah's eyes brightened again, and he grabbed Jake with a bear hug lifting him from his feet, "You found each other!" he exclaimed excitedly, then he turned to Sam and said, "All that's left is your sister and the family would be united again."

Sam and Jake looked at each other with surprise. "What do you mean?" asked Sam.

"Oh, I will explain everything," said Isaiah. "Come. Come. Let's sit in the roofed hall and I will tell you all you need to know. Have you eaten?" he asked as he led the way through the ruins towards a rock structure that was still standing.

Chapter 14
Home

Isaiah sat on the wooden chair with a large rectangular wooden table in front of him. On his right and left sat Sam and Jake on the wooden benches with their hands on the table. They had just finished eating the meat that Isaiah had prepared for them and eaten the fruits and cheeses. Zeus was sitting on the floor by Sam, gnawing on a large bone. "It all happened long ago," started Isaiah, "...when our tribe was still small. We were the strongest tribe without contender as we had been blessed by the old gods with the ability to summon exquisite weapons from thin air. Our chiefs understood the value of these weapons as they only appear when you are in real danger and can only be summoned with good intentions, even if those intentions meant killing. The tribe used these weapons to build an awesome kingdom from rock and shaped the very earth to accommodate our life. But within the tribe was a small faction that wanted to use these weapons to conquer the world. They would argue this point openly in the tribal gatherings and urge our people to become raiders. But the elders never gave in to them until, that snake Mak and his red-headed she-devil showed up. They never had our abilities, but they had our empathy. They showed up at the brink of death being chased by another tribe. They said it was because they were accused of something that no one could prove. Our elders took pity on them and brought them into our midst. They were very kind and charming at first, winning over many people's hearts. Then, during one of the tribal assemblies, Mak stood and announced that he has sent word to the nearest tribe telling them we will be attacking them. The council went crazy and wanted to banish them. But at that moment, the danger horn sounded. The tribe that was threatened decided to act first as a surprise move. Our tribe met the invaders at the gate and squashed them in a matter of minutes. But with that, we had robbed the neighboring tribe of all its men. So, we had to annex their village to ours. With this came more food for everyone, more success for businesses and of course, more support for Mak. A few weeks past and the danger horn sounded again, and just like the previous time, our tribe grew further. This went on for a while until we had more enemies than allies in our hinterland. So, the council convened and decided that the chief was too weak to put an end to Mak's activities and voted him out of his position. Obviously, he was angry about it and as he stormed out of the council hall, he announced that he will be leaving this land. Little did they know what he had in store for them." Isaiah stopped talking and got up to walk out.

A minute later, Isiah came back to the hall carrying a large flagon of ale. He put it on the table, filled his goblet and that of Sam and Jake and sat down. He took a good gulp and continued, "The council was in session for about a full day debating who should lead the tribe. Eventually, they agreed on one man. He was one of the strongest warriors in the tribe and at the same time helped anyone in need. He was known to be kind and generous with his time for mending fences, building houses and even thatching roofs. That man was your father," he said, looking at Sam. "His name was Jo," Isaiah continued, "and he had the same purple eyes you have. Jo accepted the position of chief and his first decision was to banish Mak and the she-devil that came with him. Mak left and with him, too a few men loyal to him. Jo was a good chief and the tribe prospered under his rule. The tribe loved him, and he loved them back. One pretty lady from the tribe caught his attention. She was a tall strong woman and from the highlands. Her name was Pen. Jo and Pen fell deeply in love and decided to marry. The whole tribe had a three-day wedding for them. After all, it was the chief and the most beautiful woman in the tribe. The tribe had built a house on top of a hill near here as a gift to Jo and Pen. The house was near a cliff which overlooked the whole tribal grounds and they said that they felt safer knowing Jo kept an eye on them. For six years the tribe prospered and so did Jo and Pen. They had a son and after two years they had a daughter, both with purple eyes."

Isiah stopped as his voice started breaking and felt like he was going to cry looking at Sam's purple eyes and remembering the flourishing days of the tribe. He downed the ale in his goblet and refilled it as he resumed the story. "Jo had a brother," Isaiah started. "His name was Ron. Ron and Jo would sit in silence and then both laugh as if they shared a joke. Everyone believed that these two could be having a conversation through telepathy. Ron was always there for Jo and vice versa. Ron was the architect for Jo and Pen's house. Anyway, Ron always went out of the tribe grounds to see if there is any news Jo needs to know about. He was friendly with all the gate guards and would always stop and talk to them on his way in and update them on what he saw. One day, Ron galloped through the gate without even looking at the guards. The head guardsman was concerned so he ordered the gate shut. Ron went straight to where Jo was an told him that he saw a massive army making its way to the tribe lands. Jo took this seriously and ordered the men to be ready at the gates. They waited for half a day, but nothing happened. Jo sent scouts who confirmed the presence of an army in a large clearing an hours' ride way, but their tent doors faced away from the tribe lands. This meant they are not coming for us. Then the stand down decision was taken." Isaiah drank the last of his ale and got up to stretch his body as he had been sitting in the wooden chair longer than he was accustomed to.

Isaiah walked around the room and then motioned to the men to follow him outside where he stretched further and then sat on a rock in the clearing near the hall they came out of. "When the stand down decision was taken, the tribe went back to normal life," Isaiah continued his story, "everyone went about their business and Jo went back home to build the crib for his daughter. But Ron was sure an attack would be imminent, and he went home to get his family ready to leave the tribe lands if an attack happened when no one was ready. A few days went by and things were fine. Then six riders were spotted riding into the tribe grounds from the north side where we always took the land to be a natural barrier. They rode straight to Jo and Pen's house. By the time we got there, we saw four dead riders and Jo and Pen dead. Both of them had black arrows with yellow feathers embedded in them. We knew this was the work of Mak and the she-devil. But we could not find a trace of their children. Then the alarm horn sounded and the army that was camped an hour away was at the gate with far more warriors than we could handle. The tribe fought bravely but was slaughtered. I ran to the closest village only to find everyone dead. As I turned to go through the forest to the second village, I saw Ron run with his wife and son." He turned to Jake. "You, Kahl," he said. Isaiah took a deep breath and continued, "I went to the gate village through the woods to see the old chief sitting on a horse smiling, as he announced that the tribe is his again to rule. I turned and left knowing that even killing him will do nothing. I planned to come here and bury the dead. On my way, I saw a little boy run from the healer's burning house with a bottle in his hand, he reached into the bottle, got the goo out, rubbed the wound on his thigh and passed out. I got closer to see it was Sam. I carried you," he said looking at Sam, "back here and stopped only to destroy the bridge so no one could come after you. You stayed with me for about ten years until you turned fifteen and then you decided to leave to find your sister. I have not heard from you since. That was five years ago," Isaiah's voice began breaking again as he fought back his tears. "I hid you from the world, my boy," said Isaiah, "but you will take it by storm."

Then Isiah cleared his throat and said, "A short while later, Mak and the she-devil came back and took a large house in the outer villages. They had a baby girl with them. No one knew who she was, and she spent years living in isolation in that house. One day, after you left, a beautiful young blond woman with purple eyes walked out of the house with a golden tail-lace. Only I knew who she was and have kept it to myself until today. It's your sister, Jemma." As Isaiah finished speaking, Sam heard a familiar whooshing sound coming from behind him. He instinctively moved his head to the left and raised his hand with his fingers closing shut on a black arrow with yellow feathers. The three men jumped to their feet with Sam still holding the arrow in his hand. A second arrow flew through the air and missed its mark, landing a short distance in front of the three men. Zeus looked in a direction and started growling. "Come and face us," called out Isaiah, "or are you still hiding in the shadows as usual, she-devil?" he boomed. A bush moved in the distance and the grey-haired woman Sam and Jake had met at the elder's house walked out.

"You have been on borrowed time, boy, now it's time you die," she said releasing an arrow aimed at Sam. Before Sam could react, a green light flew in front of him shattering the oncoming arrow. Sam already knew what had happened and rushed at the woman as the blue axe materialized in his hand. The grey-haired woman notched the arrow as Sam swung his axe, but she didn't have time to draw, and she released her last breath slumping to the ground holding the bow in one hand and a notched arrow in the other.

Chapter 15
The Way Back

The villages were quiet when Sam, Jake and Isaiah passed them on the way to the Chief's residence. It was barely shafaq and most of them were either waking up or having breakfast, as the aroma of coffee filled the air. The sentry posted at the gate of the Chief's house stood fast as the three men approached him, but he trembled when he saw Zeus emerge from behind Sam.

"We are here to see Gobon," said Isaiah with his deep voice, "tell him to come out and meet us."

Being terrified by Zeus and wanting to get to safety, the sentry turned and walked hurriedly into the house. A few minutes later, Gobon walked out and was surprised to see Sam and Jake there. "Surprised?" asked Sam, "Or were you expecting her?" he added as he threw a bow onto the ground in front of Gobon. The look on Gobon's face told them everything they wanted to know. "This is my land," he screamed. "Guards! Guards!" he called out. About twenty armed men ran and formed a line between Gobon and the three men. Gobon's loud calls also gathered the men from the village his house was in. The men just stood there and watched what would unfold. "You sent her to kill us," said Sam calmly, "why?"

Gobon stood there saying nothing, feeling safe behind his wall of men and their metal swords. "Answer me," shouted Sam suddenly, making Gobon and the twenty men flinch. Then Gobon spoke, "You come here hiding behind the lie that you want Isaiah to train your dog when I know you are trying to rally the people against me," he said with arrogance, "but I will not have a purple-eyed freak like you take my power away." As he mentioned Sam's eyes, a murmur erupted where the older men from the village stood, and Isaiah spoke to them. "This is Sam," he said. "Son of Jo," he added as he raised the small tail-lace Sam had showed him. "He is one of us and a high born and as such has the right to challenge the chief," he ended. Gobon looked at the tail-lace from a distance and said, "How do we know it's real, and that Jo's son lives?"

"Because I say so," said Isaiah.

"So do I," came a voice from the growing crowd watching, "and I" came another "and I" came a third, until many voices called the same thing out.

"Well, I will not have it," said Gobon. "Kill them," he ordered the guards.

Gobon's eyes widened when he saw a bright blue axe materialize in Sam's hand and a green bow in Jake's. The first of the guards to get close was sliced in half by the axe, the second decapitated by Zeus and the third slumped with a green arrow of light piercing his heart. The rest of the guards took steps backwards before running off.

"Cowards!" called out Gobon after them, but he went completely silent when Sam stood in front of him with axe in hand and Zeus growling in his face. Gobon fell to the floor crying without saying a word. Then turned up to Sam and said, "Please have mercy. I will be good. I can change. I promise."

Sam interrupted him saying, "You are asking the wrong person," Then he turned to the crowd of onlookers that was growing by the minute and said loudly, "Your fate is in their hands, for you have wronged them and have been a greedy and uncaring chief."

Turning to the crowd he said, "Do what you deem just." Sam walked off as the crowd become a mob and charged at Gobon. Sam, Jake and Isaiah left the mob and walked to the well in the center of the village where Jake pulled the bucket from the well and they all drank the cool water. "Now that Gobon is gone," asked Jake, "…what will happen here?"

Isaiah sighed a long sigh and said, "The council of elders will meet and decide who will be the next chief. Gobon was never elected, but he was selected by the old chief's dying words. The tribes had to accept a dying man's wish even though he was a vile man," he ended.

"On this note, we will need to start our journey back to Kiaff to my sister's wedding," said Sam trying the words 'my sister' in his mouth. "And we don't want to keep her majesty waiting," added Jake with a light laugh. "It is too late in the day to start your journey," said Isaiah, "and it's been an eventful morning. Stay for the day and you can leave in the morning."

By shafaq of the next day, Sam's and Jake's horses were rested, fed and watered in front of Isaiah's house. Isaiah had bid them farewell the night before to join the council of elders to find the next chief. "It will take them a while," said Jake pointing with his head towards the tribal council house. "We

140

best not wait and get moving." Sam nodded and they both mounted their horses and slowly started their journey to Kiaff which was the first stop along the way. When they got to the path to the mountain, they saw it was covered with clouds which signified a blizzard was raging up there. They prepared their jackets and started their climb on the path they took down. When they reached the point where their uphill became downhill, the weather had cleared and they looked around intently for the sabretooth, but they could not find it. They made it to the cave in the mountain by nightfall. Sam sat next to Zeus petting him and asking him if he remembered that this is where they met.

"Imagine he answered you," said Jake joking. "That would freak me out!" he ended.

The night was cold, but this time Jake was prepared with a heavy blanket he had acquired from Isiah's house with his permission. Sam was not worried as Zeus snuggled next to him keeping him warm all night. By the morning they continued their journey down the mountain, and by late afternoon, they got to the leveled ground leading to Kiaff. Being tired from the journey, Sam and Jake decided to set camp for a while for the horses to rest and for them to fill their stomachs. By the time they had started back on their journey, the second sun had set. A short while later, they could see the lights of the gates. As they drew nearer to the lights on the wall, they heard someone call and guards showed up atop the gate with their arrows notched.

"Who goes there?" shouted one guard.

"We are friends of Diapso," replied Jake, hoping it works this time again. "Who?" came the answer from the guards, making Sam and Jake's hearts stop for a second.

"Diapso," called out Jake again.

"Is that Sam and Jake?" came the response.

"Yes," answered Sam. The gate opened and out walked a guard in full gear. "Welcome to Kiaff," said Diapso as he approached, "I was told you left through this gate and hoping to see you again, I asked to be stationed here," he said with excitement. "Come, come, let's get you inside." Sam and Jake joined the guards at the gate where they heard about Lori's news. She had made it to Sanctuary and stayed a while with Lya and Serma where they asked her to look after the tavern with Serma. Diapso was so proud of his little sister becoming a partner in such a famous establishment, and he felt he owed it to Sam and Jake for saving her from the bandits. By shafaq, the bugle sounded, and the guards got ready to the change of shifts. Once the official change of guard's ceremony was done, Sam and Jake joined the night guards on their way to the barracks where they were greeted by the old timer there. The travelers stayed with the guards for breakfast and then took their leave to continue their journey to Vegna.

The first part of the journey was through the fields of Kiaff where Jake noticed that harvesting season should be very close, "Maybe by the next full moon," he guessed. As they got closer to the central circle of Kiaff, they saw the building become larger and the roads wider. Sam felt that he preferred living in the open more as he started feeling boxed in with all these buildings around him. By midday, they had reached the shop that sold them the food that you take with you, so they dismounted and ordered the same thing. The lady in the window remembered them and asked them of their journey. "We visited family," Sam said with a smile as Jake wolfed down his food. They also got Zeus some food as the

142

lady stared at him with awe and a tinge of fear. After their meal, Sam and Jake continued their journey in Kiaff with people moving out of the way or running to the side when they see Zeus walking by Sam's horse. By nightfall, they had almost made to Paul's inn when two guards stopped them. "You are in violation of the law," said one of them. "You are walking an unleashed maneater. You will pay the fine and the beast will be put to death."

Sam dismounted and walked over to the guard who was now trembling as Sam hulked above him, "You will not touch a hair on Zeus," he said, "we are going to the inn to sleep and in the morning we will leave. Any deviation from this plan will cost lives that need not be shed," he ended with his teeth clenched.

"Yes sir," said the guard and rushed off followed by the other guard who stumbled twice in his run after his friend. Without saying another word, Sam got back on his horse, and they continued to the inn. Paul almost jumped out of his clothes when he saw Zeus walk in with Sam and the people in the tavern all jumped to one side. Sam, paying no attention to the reaction Zeus was getting walked over to Paul and confirmed that his room was available; he and Zeus climbed the stairs to the room and shut the door behind them. A few minutes later, Sam went down to join Jake for dinner. Paul came over with their order and as sweetly as he could, said to Sam, "You are welcome to stay as long as you want, but the maneater with you cannot stay. There is a law against it."

"We will leave in the morning," said Sam sternly. "So, your request will be met in a few hours. Is that fine with you?"

Paul, realizing that any answer other than yes might cause him bodily harm, simply nodded and smiled. "They really fear

Zeus here, don't they?" asked Jake rhetorically. Sam nodded and ate his food in silence. After a few ales, Sam's mood brightened a bit and was more conversational with Jake. They were both getting to know each other as cousins now and the bond between them was getting much stronger. Around midnight, they decided they needed to rest for the second leg of their journey in the morning towards Sanctuary. Jake was excited to see Lya again and Sam kept his thoughts of Serma to himself.

The shafaq saw Sam and Jake leaving Kiaff in the direction of Sanctuary. They decided to take the shortcut again, so as to meet with their ladies sooner. They rode at a faster rate this time and made it to the river in record time. They took a small break allowing the horses and Zeus to rest and drink and then crossed the river at the same spot they did the time before. They had not solved the mystery of the giant snake but somehow, they felt they will encounter it again sometime in the future. By mid-day, they had made it to the second point where they needed to cross the river. Blandi was still sitting there on the same rock when they got there. "I see you are back Sam, son of Jo, and Kahl, son of Ron," he said.

"How do you know all this?" asked Sam with irritation. "I told you; I have seen what was, what is and what might be," answered Blandi with a smile exposing his rotten teeth. "How did you see it," asked Jake. "Now that's a question many have asked. The answer comes with a price you cannot pay, my boy," answered Blandi. Jake pulled out his coin pouch and shook it making a rattling sound for Blandi to know that he can pay.

"Name your price," said Jake.

"Money means nothing to me, boy," said Blandi. "The price is letting me see again for a few minutes with your eyes."

"How can you see with my eyes?" asked Jake.

"What gives me a minute of light gives you a lifetime of darkness," said Blandi, "I take your eyes and see with them as they turn to dust. In return you get the knowledge I have." Jake was considering the thought when Sam looked at him and said, "No, Jake. No!" Jake then snapped out of the temptation of ultimate knowledge. "I think I will keep my eyes to see my way," said Jake.

"A wise decision indeed!" Smiled Blandi. "Safe journey to Vegna," he ended. Sam and Jake continued their journey to Sanctuary, planning to ride well into the night to make it there before the next day.

About midnight, Sam, Jake and Zeus walked into the tavern. Only a few people were left and most of them were drunk or falling asleep. Seeing Zeus first, Lori screamed, waking up the sleepy and jolting the drunks into sobriety. Lya and Serma ran to her to see what the matter was, and they saw Jake and Sam. Lya ran and jumped into Jake's arms holding his head and kissing him passionately. Serma tried to control her walk towards Sam who rushed at her, grabbed her from the waist and lifted her above his head while looking into her eyes. He then set her down and kissed her. She kissed him back but then stepped back being shy. "Oh!" said Sam, "So sorry, you were in my mind the whole time and in my head, we had a whole relationship," he blushed. Serma stepped closer to Sam and kissed him again, "I had the same thing, this is why I was not sure if I ran to you or you to me," she said blushing. They kissed again, passionately. Lori was still terrified of Zeus who sat quietly by Sam.

"Don't worry, Lori," said Sam, "he is a gentle giant. Here, come pet him." Lori was absolutely frozen with fear and Serma went to her and held her hand drawing her closer to Sam and Zeus. As Serma reached out to pet Zeus for Lori to see, the beast wagged its tail giving Lori a fright. But having Serma and Sam there, she braved through her fear and petted Zeus on the head. Zeus then turned on his back asking for a belly rub. Lori was too scared, but Lya and Serma happily obliged him. Then Sam grabbed a chair and sat at a table and was joined by Jake, Lya and Serma. The men told them all about their journey and how they ended up being cousins and Jemma being Sam's sister. "I wonder what the new chief will be like," said Serma after they finished telling them about Gobon.

"I hope he is a good one," said Sam, "the people seemed miserable and unable to progress with the times."

"Okay, if we are to go to Vegna and be in time for the wedding…" said Lya, "we will need to leave in the morning. So, get your sleep and be ready for an early start." Sam held Serma's hand and asked, "Would you please come with us? With me?" Serma smiled, stood from her chair and then walked around the table to where Sam sat and gently sat in his lap.

"I packed this morning," she whispered in his ear, giving Sam a wide and lasting smile. The they all got up and went to their rooms for a good night's sleep ahead of the journey to Vegna.

It was almost noon when they finally left Sanctuary. Lori had needed the help of Lya and Serma to plan the orders for the inn and tavern and they had to make sure she was in complete control before leaving her. Sam and Serma rode next to each other on their horses with Zeus in between them while Jake and Lya rode behind, chatting away as usual. By sunset, they had reached the desert edge and Sam pulled out the map to find the fastest route to the resting place. They followed the direction of the map, identifying markers along the way making the trip mostly silent with the exception of elements being called out such as: "the lone tree" by Jake or "the round rock" by Serma. As dawn neared, they could see the resting place in the horizon, and they moved quickly to avoid the heat and Sam was worried about Zeus's paws being burnt. By morning, they were inside the resting place and in their rooms. Zeus was made to stay with the horses. Sam did not object much since the stable hand saved his last horse and was overjoyed to see a wolfdog. Sam knew Zeus would be in good hands. By nightfall, the travelers were back on horseback trekking through the desert to Vegna. The trip was surprisingly short as they took another of the map's shortcuts, making them arrive at the gates of Vegna before shafaq. As they neared the gate, Ben called out to the group, "Jake and Sam, are we having a beer this time round?"

"We sure are," answered Sam.

They passed the gate of Vegna and were greeted by the jet of cold air. The group made its way to the castle where Jemma was having breakfast in the garden with Roy. Jemma got up and ran to hug Lya the minute she saw her, and Roy joined them to greet the rest.

They all sat together at the King's breakfast table to tell them of their journey. Sam and Jake told every detail of their journey, about Lori, Diapso, and Isaiah, ending with Gobon.

Jemma got up and walked round the table to Sam who also got up and she hugged him and cried. "I spent my life wishing I had a brother and you spent yours looking for me, your sister," she said holding him tight.

"If I could choose, I would have chosen you," said Sam tearing up as well.

Then Jake joined them and said, "cousins," making all laugh. "Alright," said Roy, petting Zeus who was now laying between him and Sam, "dry up your tears, we have a wedding to get to!"

Epilogue

The wedding guests were milling in the garden and Sam was sitting next to Serma holding her hand. Jake and Lya were with them as they waited for the bride to walk to the reception. They got up and clapped for her while her husband, the King, walked beside her down the steps into the garden grounds. The well-wishers gathered round them and wished them a prosperous future. The King and Queen made their way to where Sam, Serma, Jake and Lya stood. "Congratulations, your majesties," said Jake, bowing. A move everyone copied.

Jemma laughed and turned to Roy saying, "This will need some time getting used to."

The King smiled for a second, then his face went very serious as he saw a large, bearded man walk into the garden, making his way to where they stood.

"Sam," said the King, "be ready. This looks like trouble." Sam got up and looked around to see Isaiah walking fast towards him. Isaiah paid no attention that anyone else was there or to the guards who were coming after him. "Isaiah!" shouted Sam waving. "Stand down!" ordered the King for the guards to let Isaiah be. When Isaiah got there, he grabbed the drink from Sam's hand and downed it. "It was a nightmare to get you," he said to Sam breathlessly, "the council has voted for a new chief. It's you!" he ended.

Then he turned to Jemma and his eye immediately watered, "Oh my precious girl, how beautiful you have become." Then realizing she is now the queen, he bowed deeply and said, "Your majesty."

Jemma smiled and blushed at the same time and said, "For what you have done to my family, it is I that must bow to you," and softly bowed her head.

Isaiah smiled then turned to Sam and said, "You must come to the free tribes and be the chief of legend, the one who will make us glorious again."

Sam turned to Serma, who said, "I can be ready in an hour."